SABOTAGE

THE LEAGUE OF MARITIME ADVENTURERS

BOOK TWO

SABOTAGE

Steve Wedlock

and

Steve Dean

Text: Steve Wedlock and Steve Dean
Editor: Gail Kathryn Swift
Cover and Interior Illustrations: Raphael Quek
Cover and Interior Design & Layout: Danielle Smith-Boldt

ISBN 978-1-7379854-2-6 (Paperback)
ISBN 978-1-7379854-3-3 (eBook)

TABLE OF CONTENTS

SABOTAGE

All supplies very bad and dear, and there are no facilites
for even the smalles repairs.—Sailing Directions.

HER nationality was British, but you will not find her house-flag in the list of our mercantile marine. She was a nine-hundred-ton, iron, schooner-rigged, screw cargo-boat, differing externally in no way from any other tramp of the sea. But it is with steamers as it is with men. There are those who will for a consideration sail extremely close to the wind; and, in the present state of a fallen world, such people and such steamers have their use. From the hour that the *Aglaia* first entered the Clyde— new, shiny, and innocent, with a quart of cheap champagne trickling down her cut-water—Fate and her owner, who was also her captain, decreed that she should deal with embarrassed crowned heads, fleeing Presidents, financiers of over-extended ability, women to whom change of air was imperative, and the lesser law-breaking Powers. Her career led her sometimes into the Admiralty Courts, where the sworn statements of her skipper filled his brethren with envy. The mariner cannot tell or act a lie in the face of the sea, or mis-lead a tempest; but, as lawyers have discovered, he makes up for chances withheld when he returns to shore, an affidavit in either hand.

From: "THE DEVIL AND THE DEEP SEA"
by Rudyard Kipling

FOREWORD

Welcome to the League of Maritime Adventurers! This is the second book of the series. In writing this book, we hope it might encourage the exploration of the many coasts and oceans of this wonderful world of ours. By telling exciting stories and relating observations on so many interesting subjects, we seek to inform and educate in a fun and thrilling manner.

Woven through the stories, forming part of them, will be such diverse topics as: star lore and navigation, oceanography, biology, aquaculture, ecology and so many more. We hope to spark the reader's curiosity such that they ask questions – maybe even do a little "outside" research- to touch a sea urchin's needles and feel seaweed, smell a low tide and taste a scallop. Follow the exciting adventures of our crew of teenagers as they discover some of what is waiting to be discovered out there, how to protect it for future generations…

PROLOGUE

A small boat moved slowly across the calm sea on a warm summer day, its twin outboard engines chugging a deep rhythm as they pushed against the ebbing tide. Despite its appearance, and the actions of the lone occupant, this was no tourist boat. Acting as casually as possible, the figure moved closer to a red buoy floating on the slight swell. It had taken over two hours to find the buoy, despite knowing approximately where it was by observing those who placed it here. Growing anger was replaced by a sense of triumph and a wide smile.

Taking this job had been something of a necessity; there weren't many employment opportunities for an ex-con with a hot temper. Desperation, and some skill with boats, had led to the present job and a promised cash payment if everything went to plan.

To the port side, the town of Stonehaven sat among the green hills of the Maine coast. On the starboard side, several small islands could be seen, the sea in between dotted with pleasure craft of various sizes.

The buoy was anchored on a sand bank relatively close to shore, away from the regular shipping lanes and other places the many tourists usually went. The skipper steered the boat closer, double-checking no one was watching. There were other boats around, but none close enough to see what was happening. Once within range, the skipper grabbed a boat hook and fished around for the anchor line, a brown natural-fibre rope in this case. The boat moved towards the buoy and was soon alongside it. The skipper pulled enough line out of the water to grab it, then set to work.

It needed to look like an accident, as if the line had frayed and snapped. With a razor blade, the skipper began to make random cuts in the individual strands of the rope. It soon parted and the person stepped away, letting both ends fall back into the sea. Freed from its anchor, the buoy began to drift away from its position. Job done.

The skipper moved the boat away from the anchor and the buoy, steering as casually as before, and turning in a vague homeward direction. Although the skipper didn't fully understand what was going on here, it was easy money, and they had been promised more jobs like this.

CHAPTER ONE
SEA POWER

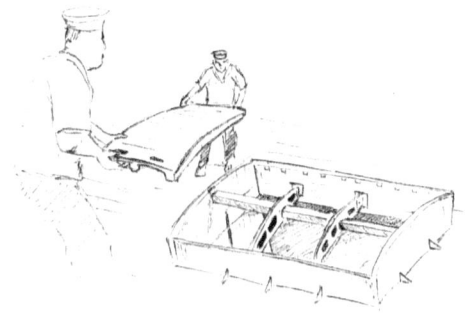

BATTEN DOWN THE HATCHES

If a ship was expecting bad weather, the crew would
batten down the hatches to stop water getting into the hold.
The hatches or cargo access points were covered in canvas
and fixed down with battens or lengths of wood.

The modern meaning is of someone preparing for any
difficult situation, which could be an actual event
or a change in circumstances.

As evening approached, a small boat skipped over the ocean with five teenagers aboard, returning from a picnic on Bear Cub Island. They were heading back to the harbor and then home after their first full day together this summer. They'd decided to start their vacation as they had planned at the end of last summer, and actually use the boat to have some fun instead of just sitting in it while it was tied to the jetty.

Their small boat had seen better days, but they'd recently been taking better care of it and using it more. Officially, it was called the *Peggy Sue* but time and salt water hadn't been kind to the paintwork and it was now known affectionately as the *'eggy Su'*. It actually belonged to a relative, who'd gone to South America on a backpacking tour, but they'd been down there for over four years now.

Conner Allen took his usual place at the helm. He was 15 now, 5 foot 6 and growing like a weed. His rapid growth had left him slim of build, despite his ravenous appetite. He had gray eyes and black hair, which he kept short to stop it blowing into his eyes out at sea. Being a teenager, his clothing was mostly black or dark shades of other colors. Today, he was wearing jeans, a plain black t-shirt, and black and gray trainers. A dark gray jacket was balled up on the seat beside him, and a small bag sat between his feet.

"What's that?" asked Terry, who, always on lookout duty because of his sharp eyes, stood slightly and pointed off to the starboard side a short distance ahead. "Something red, looks like a buoy but it's drifting."

Terry Shay was a Native American of the Penobscot tribe. Although he was also 15, his growth spurt had yet to kick in fully, and he was barely 5 foot 4 tall. He had dark black shoulder-length hair, brown eyes and olive-brown skin. He was of thin build, although he was starting to widen across the shoulders. As usual, he was wearing several layers of clothing, despite the warmth. They consisted of hard-wearing items, mostly green. Folded up under his seat was a long coat in dark green. It had dozens of pockets, most of them filled with everything he needed for the day, possibly several days.

Conner steered the boat in the direction Terry was pointing, moving slowly to avoid getting too close. The red object was soon in sight. Jenna and Ryan, who both sat on the starboard side, Jenna in front, tried to work out what it was. Jenna Cushman was the oldest of the group at almost sixteen, of average build, 5 foot 5 with brown eyes and light brown hair. She was dressed in a loose white shirt, red canvas jeans and her trademark orange trainers. Her hair had been cut short over the winter and barely touched her shoulders.

"It looks like a marker buoy," Jenna said, "but there's something attached to it. Move closer."

Conner nudged the throttle and moved the boat to within a few feet of the object.

Ryan shaded his eyes against the sun to get a better view. "It looks like some kind of monitoring equipment, definitely some electronics in there. Let's get it on board."

Ryan McNeal was Conner's best friend. He was ahead in the growth race at about 5 feet 7, noticeably wider than Conner and had short, light brown hair and light gray eyes. He was dressed all in black as usual, a t-shirt, jeans and trainers, and a black leather jacket that was older than him.

"You sure it's safe, Ry?" Dawn asked from the opposite side of the boat. She was Ryan's younger sister, now 14 and barely 5 feet tall. She hadn't really grown in any direction, much to her frustration. She had the same light gray eyes as Ryan, and long blonde hair tied in a braid that reached the small of her back. She was wearing blue jeans and a white t-shirt with a bald eagle on it, white trainers and was holding a yellow jacket in her lap.

The buoy was already on board by the time Ryan had reacted to his sister's question. "Looks safe to me."

Conner, Ryan and Dawn lived in the town of Stonehaven the whole year round, opposite each other on the same street. Conner with his parents and younger sister, Ryan and Dawn with their dad, stepmom and older sister. They'd all been born here and went to school together. Terry and Jenna both lived inland and spent the summer, June to September, on the coast. Terry's family lived several miles inland, but moved to what they called their "artists' retreat" on the coast during the summer. His dad made sculptures of animals and his mom made large oil paintings.

Jenna's parents had divorced some years ago, so she'd moved to the town with her mother and three older sisters, who now all lived with their mom's mom in a small house. During the winter, the girls all went to their dad's place, a large apartment in Washington D.C. and a million miles away from small town life. The five had all met while taking part in the volunteer program and immediately become friends. Since then, they'd spoken or texted almost every day. Even when they were apart, they chatted via text or video-call, and often played online games together.

Now they could see it better, the object turned out to be something of a mystery to them, and not something they'd seen before. It consisted of three units; the buoy, a plastic box with electronics inside and a solid plastic lump that was covered in resin. A red LED was glowing on the electronics, so something was still working. The box was attached to the buoy by a steel cable, which seemed to be spring-loaded. The resin lump hung down underneath it all, suspended from the box by a chain with a cable woven through it. A frayed piece of rope was all that remained of what they assumed was the anchor line. There were no markings on it, but it looked expensive and someone was probably looking for it.

"We can ask around when we get back," Conner said. "Maybe post some photos online, see if anyone recognises it."

"On it," Dawn said, her phone out and already framing the shot. Although they all had phones, they couldn't get a signal this far out at sea, so they tended not to pay too much attention to them once they were beyond the breakers.

A short while later, they entered Stonehaven Harbor and were soon moored up to the jetty in their designated berth. The small and ancient outboard engine fell silent and they all climbed out, Ryan passing the buoy up to the others. They had intended to carry the contraption around to the Harbormaster's office, but as they crossed the parking lot someone called out to them.

A man and a woman were standing beside an old green four-wheel drive vehicle with a kayak on the roof rack and another on the ground beside them. The couple were in their mid- twenties. The man was of Hispanic origin, tall and dark haired with brown eyes; the woman was also dark haired and her eyes were a deep chocolate. She had similar skin color to Terry, but wasn't a Native American, as far as they could tell. They were both wearing blue wetsuits, and obviously going or coming back from kayaking.

"Hello!" the man said, "we were just about to go looking for that."

"It's yours?" Conner asked.

"Yes, it went missing sometime over the last few days."

"What is it?" Ryan asked, partly because he was interested and partly as a test of ownership.

"It's a prototype wave generator. A scale model at least. It's supposed to be collecting data out at sea." The man leaned over and examined the anchor line. "I don't like the look of that; it shouldn't have frayed so much in just a few days."

"Maybe something's been chewing on it," Conner suggested.

"That's why we used natural-fiber rope to be safe. We might have to rethink that one. Could you just put it in the trunk for us? It doesn't look too damaged."

The children carried it over to the couple's car and the woman opened the trunk. Inside were several similar pieces of equipment and some more of the buoys. The kids were convinced they'd found the rightful owners.

"My name is Matias, this is my wife, Teuila." The woman's name sounded like 'Twila'.

They exchanged greetings and all introduced themselves.

"Where did you find it?" Teuila asked, examining the buoy.

"It was just floating in the sea about half a mile out, maybe less. We were coming back from Bear Cub Island and were heading straight for the harbor entrance, so somewhere around there," Conner answered, looking to Terry to confirm.

"You have a boat?" Matias asked.

"Yes. The 'eggy Su', it's the old twenty-footer tied to the jetty."

"Interesting. We only have these kayaks. They're good fun, but not at all practical for transporting our equipment."

"We didn't really think that one through!" Teuila laughed.

"We could help," Conner volunteered. "We're off school, homework's all...well, mostly done. We're quite experienced when it comes to maritime stuff."

The couple both smiled widely. "You are?" Matias asked. "That's good to know. And I suppose you're very familiar with the local area, land and sea?"

"We are," Conner nodded. "Me, Ryan and Dawn have lived here all our lives. Terry and Jenna come here every summer. We've been messing around in boats since we were little."

"We had quite an adventure last summer," Jenna said proudly. "We found some people were dumping plastic waste in the sea. We stopped it; and we rescued one of the smugglers."

"That was you? Amazing." Teuila smiled. "We read about it when we were researching the area."

"You did a good job; I wish everyone was as keen as you. We need to look after the oceans; and I think what we're doing might make people appreciate them more," Matias said seriously.

"What, exactly, are you doing?" Ryan asked, looking over the other stuff in the trunk.

"We're working on a project to produce electricity from the sea, specifically from waves." Matias said. When Ryan showed greater interest, Matias showed them how it all worked.

"The buoy floats and goes up and down with the waves. The anchor holds these two parts, this mass here is actually a battery, and the generator and all the electronics are in the box. When a wave lifts or lowers the buoy, it drives the generator which charges the battery. The idea is to scale it up and have a system where the batteries are swapped out when they're full and are replaced with discharged ones. So, no power cables messing up the sea bed, just a boat to swap them out, which can be a robot and also be battery powered. And the tides are reliable and predictable, which wind and solar aren't."

"That's pretty clever!" Ryan nodded in approval.

"Well, it would have been. It all depends on wave height and how regular it is. We'll have to see if we can get any useful data off it when we plug it into the PC."

"Thank you for finding this," Teuila said. "We're running to a tight budget and these things aren't cheap." She smiled, wide and bright. The boys smiled back, but seemed unable to speak. The girls shared a look, rolling their eyes.

"Yes, thanks, we owe you a favor. We're renting a cottage nearby, number 23 on Mason Road, the white one with the outbuildings. If you find anything else, or need anything, feel free to visit."

"Yes, we will. Thanks," Jenna said.

"Good luck," Dawn added.

The children headed off home, through the side streets and back alleys of Stonehaven. They walked past the dumpster that had kicked off the events of last year. Despite Jenna's short description of the events, it had actually taken a good portion of the summer and a lot of hard work to find out what was happening and who was involved. They'd managed to keep their names off the local news, mainly due to their ages, and had been referred to as 'local teens'; but some people knew who they were and what they'd done.

"He never did thank us," Ryan said as they continued on.

"Marty Whitford? No, he didn't."

"You'd think he'd be grateful we saved his life," Dawn said.

"I heard he's having to sell his trawler to pay his fine and legal bills," Jenna said.

"Maybe that's why he hasn't thanked us," Terry pointed out. "He probably blames us for what happened to him."

"We didn't make him do it," Conner insisted, "it was his choice."

"He was never much of a fisherman anyway," Ryan added.

Dawn went over and looked into the dumpster. "Half full. I guess nothing changes after all." The waste they'd found was mostly bubble wrap, which was used in large quantities in Stonehaven, but wasn't easily recycled. Some of it washed up on the beach while they were cleaning it as part of their volunteer work. They'd found more right here, exactly the same, and that had started their adventure.

Terry frowned. "It's going to be left to our generation to sort it out, and we can't even vote yet."

"It will be too late by the time anything's done about it," Dawn replied.

"Don't be so negative." Jenna put her arm around Dawn's shoulders. "We made a difference last year. We stopped that stuff going into the sea at least. And there are only five of us. Imagine what we could do if the whole town pulls together, or the whole world."

"That's not going to happen," Dawn frowned, "some people care more about money than the planet they live on."

"Ok, the whole world of people under twenty-five."

This early in the evening, Stonehaven was busy with traffic and pedestrians. It was a tourist destination and many people had summer properties here. The rich folks owned private islands in the bay, the less rich had condos on the sea front, and the normal people lived in the more modest houses further inland. It wasn't a beach destination as such, although the town did have a very nice one. Most people came for sea-related activities like wind-surfing, messing around in boats, and fishing. Lately, people were commenting, the fishing hadn't been so good.

They reached Conner's and Ryan and Dawn's houses first. Jenna carried on around the corner and down the street to her grandmother's house. Terry had the furthest to walk as his family-owned house was on the far edge of Stonehaven. Conner had barely got inside his front door before the texts started coming in. Remarks were made about Teuila, which the boys all strenuously denied, and then the topic turned to more normal teenage fare.

CHAPTER TWO

AROUND THE ISLAND

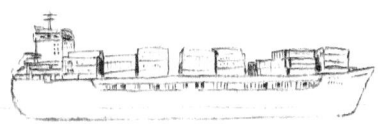

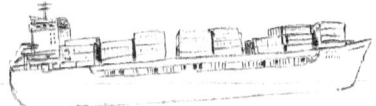

ON AN EVEN KEEL

*Any boat or ship will move easier through the water
if the whole keel is sitting level in the water and not higher
at one end or leaning to one side.*

*In modern times it's come to mean keeping or making
a situation calm and steady during uncertain times
or changing events.*

Early the next morning, Conner left his house and met up with Ryan and Dawn as they emerged from theirs. Although neither of them said anything, Conner could tell they'd been bickering again. They were actually very close, or at least had been, until, as Jenna's gran put it, hormones had happened. Dawn's dad and stepmom were very protective of her and only allowed her the freedom she had if Ryan was there. For some reason, Dawn blamed Ryan for this and often took it out on him. Ryan, for his part, mostly ignored her complaints in his own stoic way. Sometimes he would make a sarcastic comment and then things would kick off. Luckily, once they were all together, they were generally more friendly.

The three took their usual route across town and down to the harbor. They were talking about the game they'd all played online last night, as a team and against each other. This, pizza, movies, and music were the main topics of conversation on most summer days.

As usual, Terry was already there when they arrived at the jetty. He was, also as usual, playing a game on his phone. Unlike most teenagers, Terry liked to get up early to make the most of the day. He was lying across one of the seats, feet up on the gunwale and seemingly totally immersed in his game. The others knew different. No one had ever managed to sneak up on him, even if it looked like he was asleep.

As if to prove this point, Terry gestured to a red gas can sitting on the jetty before the others were within twenty feet of the boat. "There's a message."

Conner walked over to the gas can and shook it. "It's full."

There was a note tucked under the handle, a page torn out of a notebook. Written on it was a series of numbers and underneath those a signature. Conner showed it to the others.

"That looks like GPS coordinates," Ryan said.

"BoatProf? Isn't that the guy you told us about, the one who wrote the book?" Dawn asked.

During last summer's adventure, they'd received some small but very useful gifts from a kind stranger. It turned out the old book of maritime knowledge Conner's parents had given him had been written by the same man. This mysterious individual called himself the BoatProf. Conner checked the pocket of his jacket to make sure the book was still there. He carried it everywhere and regularly quoted from it and tested the others by asking random questions; they learned a lot last summer from Conner doing this every time they got together.

Conner nodded, "Yes, that's him, wonder what he wants?"

"Maybe he wants to give us some work," Ryan suggested.

"That would be good," Dawn smiled.

"I'm guessing the coordinates are out at sea, as there's gas for the boat," Terry said, without taking his eyes off his phone.

Conner, Ryan and Dawn all pulled their phones out and started searching for the location.

"Yes," Conner said first. "Looks like an island, north of Bear Cub. No name given."

"It's not that far. We can get there in an hour, maybe a bit more," Ryan guessed.

"We'll have to wait for Jenna, she's gone to the store," Dawn said.

"Doing chores for her grandmother?" Conner asked.

"Yes, but she's also getting herself a new lifejacket."

"Why, what's wrong with the one she's got?" Ryan said.

"It doesn't fit her anymore." Dawn turned away and jumped into the boat.

Ryan had a puzzled look on his face. "She isn't that much taller."

"Not taller you jerk, work it out," Dawn yelled, causing Terry to look over.

Conner and Ryan were completely baffled until Conner realized what she meant. "Oh, it's tighter across the chest." He said it in a matter-of-fact way, then blushed to his hair-roots.

Ryan turned his attention to the gas can. "Yes, well, we can fuel up while we wait for her."

The gas tank was full and their route was all plotted out by the time Jenna arrived. She was carrying an orange life jacket, one of the more compact designs with adjustable straps. She was an excellent swimmer and had competed for her school; but the sea wasn't a swimming pool and it was better to be safe than sorry. They all greeted her as casually as they could and no one mentioned her new purchase. Dawn explained to her about the note and where they were going; and at the same time some unspoken message also seemed to pass between them.

Conner, as always, went through the safety check list, as recommended in his book. "So, weather's good, fuel is full, life jackets on, we should get some flares after what happened last year. And we still don't have an anchor, charts in phones. Ok, let's go."

"We should tell someone before we go," Jenna suggested, "let them know where we'll be. Better safe than sorry."

"Ok, but not my parents," Dawn pulled a face. "They won't let me go if they think it's somewhere unfamiliar."

"And not mine," Terry said, "they'll think something is wrong if I start telling them where I'm going." He smiled when he said it, but the others suspected he was only half joking.

"Ok, I'll do it." Conner pulled out his phone and the note and sent a text to his mom. "'Off to island near Bear Cub, don't know name, here's co-ords.' Send."

His phone buzzed only a few seconds later. " 'OK. Be careful, don't be late. Kiss.' Right, let's go."

The outboard engine started on the second pull and settled into a steady but irregular rumble. Apart from running out of fuel, it hadn't let them down yet, despite its age. Conner slowly headed towards the harbor entrance and the sea beyond. They all glanced over at the empty berth that once held the fishing vessel Marty Whitford had used to smuggle the plastic waste out to sea. The trawler had been sold at auction down the coast. No one knew what had happened to it after that; they doubted anyone would buy it to use as a fishing boat. All the fishermen in the area had been complaining for years about reduced catches, whether that was fish, shrimp or lobster. Over-fishing, pollution and climate change were all to blame; but, sadly, very few people appeared to be doing anything about it.

The sea was calm today, an offshore breeze blew from the west and the sun shone in a blue sky. There were vessels everywhere they looked, all shapes and sizes, from sail boards to luxury yachts to huge container ships on the horizon.

The noise of the engine prevented proper conversation, so each of the children was left with their own thoughts as Conner steered first towards Bear Cub island and then north to the mystery location. It was further away than they guessed. Despite the good weather and the calm sea, they'd already been traveling for over an hour before they were anywhere near the right place.

"Ok, we're getting close," Terry was looking at his phone.

"Wait, you've got a signal?" Dawn pulled out her phone and checked it.

Terry laughed. "No, not a phone signal, but you can still get GPS data without it, depending on your phone."

"You can?" Conner, Ryan and Jenna all said, taking out their own phones.

"Of course, the signal comes down from the satellites, which are always in range. It takes longer to update sometimes, and you can't download maps and things, obviously, but it still works."

"Is that not covered in your book, Con?" Ryan teased.

"I don't think they had satellites, never mind smart phones when that was written."

As they neared the location, they saw it was indeed an island. They'd never been further north than Bear Cub Island before, and were now wondering what else they'd missed by staying close to home. They approached the location slowly, keeping a couple of hundred yards out to sea. The western side of the island was mainly low cliffs with a few gravel inlets. Evergreen trees stood shoulder to shoulder, growing almost down to the water line. The trees cleared as they moved further north and were replaced by grassland at what turned out to be a headland. Buildings could be seen on the other side, low and mostly small.

They continued on around the headland and into a wide bay with a narrow shingle beach. They could now plainly see the buildings and a small harbor on the eastern side of the headland. This looked like it had been built over several years, with different layers of worked stone and concrete forming the jetties and quay. At the rear, a long slipway had been formed into the slope. Several small buildings, mostly wooden shacks, were clustered at the top. More substantial buildings, some of them converted shipping containers, stood further back. Moored within the protective arms of the harbor were several boats of different types and sizes. The one thing they all had in common was their condition. Every one of them was in serious need of repair. A couple of them were really low in the water and might even have been beyond rescue. The 'eggy Su' looked brand new in comparison.

They continued circumnavigating the island, around another couple of headlands, and found a long, sandy beach shaped almost like a hook. Around the south and south east sides were clusters of smaller islands, some of them not much more than rocks barely showing above the sea. When they returned to their point of origin, they guessed the island was shaped like a crooked "H", with the buildings at the top of the left upright and the sandy beach on the lower side of the crossbar.

Once they were satisfied it was safe to land, Conner headed into the harbor and over to a vacant mooring. At this point a figure appeared at the top of the slope and headed down towards them. He waved as he neared, a wide smile on his face. He looked to be in his mid-sixties, had short gray hair and sharp blue eyes. He was clean shaven, with heavily tanned skin and rosy cheeks. He was wearing the heavy-looking coat Conner had seen him in last summer, like a larger and more military version of Terry's.

"Hello everyone, welcome to my island. My name is Frank, but most people call me BoatProf, or just Prof for short." He shook hands with them all as they climbed out of the boat and gave him their names.

"What's the name of this island?" Dawn asked, notebook and pencil ready.

"Well now, that depends on who you ask and which maps you study. Officially, it's called Roque Island, sounds like rock but spelled "r o q u e". On the old maps it's called Rogue Island, which is much better in my opinion." The professor smiled widely. "Now, you might be wondering why I asked you to come here. Well, let's go and find somewhere to sit and I'll explain." The Prof turned to walk back up the slope gesturing for them to follow.

The children swapped glances and then decided to comply. They'd come this far, might as well see what it was all about.

At the top of the slope, the professor headed towards one of the buildings and pushed the door open. He waited on the threshold until they'd all caught up, then went inside. Ryan looked through the door then stepped inside, the others quickly joining him. Although small and smelling of paint and wood resin, it was pleasant enough inside. The whole building was only about five yards wide and eight yards long, with exposed rafters holding up an apex roof. The floor was solid and there was a window running almost the whole length on one side. The walls were covered in pictures of ships, parts of ships, equipment for ships, and anything generally related to ships and the things people did with them. Arranged in a single row across the back wall of the building were eight wooden desks and eight chairs, all different. It was, without doubt, a class room.

"Take a seat, anywhere you like and I'll explain." The professor smiled and gestured towards the desks. Ryan moved over and sat down, closely followed by Dawn. Conner sat the other side of Dawn and then Jenna and Terry sat beside Conner.

"Excellent!" The professor smiled. "As you might have noticed, I'm getting old. After a lifetime of maritime adventure, I've decided to settle down here and pass on my many years of experience to the next generation, which is, if you agree, yourselves."

The children nodded but didn't speak.

"As my first pupils, I will teach you free of charge and I will even give you a boat to work on. You can, again if you agree, work on the boat while learning the skills necessary to restore it to seaworthiness, and then I'll teach you how to sail it. How does that sound?"

"Sounds good," Conner replied. "You know we can only come here in the summer, and not every day?"

"Of course, and it's not a problem. There might be times when I'm not here myself, but you can come and go as you please, freely use the materials and facilities and generally have fun while learning. What do you say?"

The five exchanged a few muttered comments, then Conner spoke for them. "OK, we'll give it a try."

"Excellent! Welcome to my maritime academy! Let me show you the boat, I'll bet you're eager to get started."

The BoatProf practically skipped out of the door and headed back towards the small harbor. He stopped at the top of the slope and beamed a wide smile. "Here it is! What a beauty."

The children gathered around and looked where he was looking. They saw nothing but a pile of old wood that looked ready for the bonfire. As they stared, a shape began to appear in what they had thought was a random collection of planks. The top deck of a sailing boat lay there, with no mast and no sides. They suddenly realised the whole boat was in fact present, but very few of its parts were actually connected. If they thought the boats in the harbor were bad, this one was worse. It might have been quicker, they thought, to get a saw and start again with a tree.

"I've no idea what she's called, the name was lost long ago, but I've no doubt you'll come up with something good. They say it's bad luck to rename a ship, but I don't believe all that superstitious nonsense. I have the blueprints for this model, so you'll need to have a look at those. And don't worry, it isn't half as bad as it looks. Come on, I'll show you around."

The BoatProf headed back up the hill while the children lagged behind.

"When he said he was giving us a boat I thought it was going to be one of the sunken ones." Dawn said, shaking her head.

"Me too," Jenna pushed one of the pieces of wood with her toe, it broke.

"Me three," Ryan bent down dug around the deck piece. "It's buried, actually buried in the mud."

"Come on," Conner took a few steps after the prof, who was waiting patiently outside another building. "Let's see what else he's got around here."

The BoatProf showed them proudly around the site. Every time he opened a door it was like he was revealing a great treasure. The children had to admit the insides were more impressive than the outsides. All of the buildings were old, mismatched and patched up, obviously brought here from other places. Inside every one of them it was clean, dry and tidy. There was a small but spotless canteen, some toilet facilities, which were of the composting variety, and lots of storage spaces filled with shelves and neatly labelled.

The BoatProf saved the best until last, at least by his criteria. A huge blue shipping container stood overlooking the slipway. How it had got there he didn't say; it certainly hadn't been dismantled and shipped in sections like the rest of the buildings. The solar panels on the roof and the cable running into it from a small wind turbine gave a clue to its contents. The door opened with a creak of rusty hinges and revealed a series of machine tools arranged along one wall. The teens recognised a lathe, a band saw and a drill press, but several others were unfamiliar to them. Hanging on the opposite wall were dozens, possibly hundreds, of hand tools. Everything from a simple hammer to some exotic looking wood-shaping tools to things they had no names for.

"This place needs to be kept locked, of course, when you aren't using it. I'll give you some spare keys. The batteries, which are around the back, are pretty good but won't last indefinitely, unless it's very sunny and windy at the same time. I'll show you how to use them as the need arises."

The professor closed the door and locked it with the heavy padlock. "Ok, one last thing to show you." He headed back through the academy and beyond the last building, then down a slight hill and through a hedge of different-sized evergreen trees. "We don't waste anything here," Prof said, running his hand through the needles of one of the trees. "These are all Christmas trees people had thrown out. Some of them don't make it, but it's surprising how many do, as long as they still have their roots of course."

Beyond the hedge was a clearing, and in the center was a large houseboat. The children stopped and stared in wonder. It looked like it had been freshly delivered from the factory, with its polished wood, bright paint and spotless windows. There was a row of solar panels on the roof, gleaming in the sun, and the usual collection of antennae.

"How did this get here?" Dawn asked.

"I made it hull upwards. Do you like it?"

"You made it, all of it?" Dawn was sure he was teasing them.

"Yes, right here. I had to buy in some of the materials of course, and some of the fixtures, but most of it was made by my own hands in that workshop."

"How long did it take?" Ryan asked.

"Well, let's see. About… twelve years, on and off. I had to make a living, of course."

The children stood admiring the boat for some time.

"Come in, wipe your feet." The professor climbed the few steps that led to a deck that ran around the entire boathouse. He stopped with one hand on the door handle. "By the way, I don't live here alone. I didn't want you to be overwhelmed, so I asked my family to stay in here." With a mischievous grin he opened the door and took a step back.

To the teens, it looked like someone had opened the doors at the pound and let all the dogs out. The pack's first reaction was to mob the BoatProf. They jumped all over him, their tails wagging, until they spotted the teens. They sniffed at them for a few seconds, and then mobbed them too. Despite appearances, there were actually only six of them, no two the same. In fact, it looked like someone had deliberately chosen one of each from a dog breed chart. The teens soon realised the dogs only had ten eyes between them, nine ears, twenty-one legs and five and a half tails.

After several minutes of fuss, the prof spoke. "Ok, that's enough, go and play." The dogs all stopped, looked at him and then ran off in the same direction. "I'll introduce you to them later, but smallest to largest, that was Bowline, Reef, Diamond, Clove, Carrick and Cleat."

"Where did they all come from?" Terry asked, still watching them as they sniffed around the trees in the distance.

"They found their own way here, the flotsam and jetsam of uncaring folk who didn't know how lucky they were."

"That's terrible," Terry gasped.

"Not for me, I wouldn't part with any one of them for a chest full of gold." The professor smiled. "There's also a cat around here too, his name's Bosun. He's a big brown speckled thing, supposed to be a Maine Coon, but he's not very sociable. If you see him, let him come to you; if he rubs against your legs he likes you, then you can pet him. But don't try to pick him up or grab him in any way, he doesn't like that."

"How does he get along with the dogs?" Terry asked.

"Better than with humans, surprisingly. I often find him mixed in with the dog pile, although he makes himself scarce when they get too boisterous. Right, let's get inside. I'll make us some drinks. Tea, coffee, water? I don't have soda, I'll have to get some."

Inside, the boathouse was just as impressive, if marred slightly by piles of hairy dog blankets. They gathered in the main room, a large open space filled with enough maritime antiques to fill a sizeable store. It was overlooked by a glass-panelled wooden balcony that formed part of the second floor, and under this was a gleaming white kitchen a TV chef would have been proud of. There was an overall smell of wood and wood polish, which mostly covered the odour of wet dog.

The children each took a seat as the professor went to the kitchen and began to assemble a tray of drinks. The chairs were all the same design, but were made from different types of wood. Each had a thick cushion of dark red leather and was very comfortable.

"Did you make these as well?" Dawn asked.

The professor glanced over. "Yes, everything made of wood was designed and made by me right here on the island. Some of the things I had to buy, like the windows, and some of the fittings I bartered for, either with stuff or time. I had to get an electrician in, of course, to make sure the wiring was safe. But if I could make it, I did. It's a real vessel, you know? If the sea ever rises this far it would just float away. It's even got a prop and a motor."

He brought over a jug of iced water with slices of lemon floating in it and poured them all a glass. "So, what do you say? Do you want to be the first students of my maritime academy?"

"Yes," The children all answered simultaneously.

"Cheers!" The professor, a beaming smile on his face and a certain moisture in his eyes, held up his glass and they all clinked them together to seal the deal.

CHAPTER THREE
FIRE AND WOOD

TO FORGE AHEAD

*Not a blacksmithing term, but meaning to continue
moving forwards by the power of sails or oars.
Probably from the Italian phrase 'forza di remo / di vela.'*

*In modern times it's come to mean to keep moving
or making progress despite difficult conditions
or circumstances.*

A few days later, the children were gathered at the 'eggy Su' getting ready to go across to the BoatProf's island. They were loading up their backpacks and doing the usual checks before heading out to sea.

"Did you hear all the sirens last night?" Jenna asked as she climbed into the boat.

"I did," Dawn replied, "they woke me up."

"I didn't," Ryan grinned, "they didn't wake me up."

"Typical," Dawn sighed.

"Yeah, I heard them, what was that all about?" Conner asked.

"Big fire in a warehouse on Quarry Road, according to my gran. They didn't say who owned it on the news, or what was inside," Jenna explained.

"Quarry road is near Mason Road," Conner said, checking his phone.

"Where Matias and Teuila are living," Ryan said. "Should we go and check on them?"

"Sure, won't take long," Conner stood and climbed up onto the jetty without further encouragement. Jenna and Dawn stood watching as the boys headed off. They shook their heads and made some whispered comments, but eventually followed along.

It was a short walk north to the edge of town. This area was a mix of small, old houses and larger premises, some of them converted from one or more houses in the distant past. Most of them were made from gray stone, supplied by the industry that gave the town and many local places their names. The quarry itself had closed many years ago but its legacy remained.

They could smell the sharp odour of burning blowing on the wind as they got closer. They soon found Quarry Road, and from there the ruined building was obvious. They approached it as close as they could, a cordon had been set up around it as there was danger of what remained of the building collapsing. The warehouse was one of the few more modern buildings in the area; a steel skeleton clad in metal sheets. One end of it had been burned away completely, leaving the twisted beams exposed like the bones of a giant creature. What remained, inside and out, was a blackened mess. The children could see the many pools of water created by the fire hoses and water still trickled and dripped from the wreckage, but the firefighters were no longer here.

Matias was standing with a small group of people, talking and pointing. To the boys' disappointment, there was no sign of Teuila. The children approached the group and waited. Matias turned when he saw the other people looking and a bright smile spread across his face.

"Hello there! How are you all?"

Conner answered for the group. "Fine thanks. We heard the sirens, and thought we'd check if you were ok."

"Yes, we're good. No one was injured, but these guys have lost a lot of stuff." He turned to the other people, two men and a woman. They all had soot on their hands and boots, as if they'd been digging through the wreckage. "These fine children are locals, perhaps they can help with the investigation."

One of the men turned to them, his face serious. "Luckily it all happened overnight, as you heard, so there was no one inside. The strange thing is there was nothing in the building that could catch fire on its own, we didn't even have the power on. And as you can see, our equipment was stacked in one corner, leaving most of the warehouse empty. That's exactly where the fire started, so we're pretty sure it was arson. If you hear anything, we'd be grateful if you could let us know."

Conner nodded, "of course."

"What was in there?" Ryan asked.

The man hesitated, but then explained. "Mostly surveying equipment, measuring devices, that kind of thing. We're doing research for a power company, looking into renewable energy."

Conner nodded, "like you then, Matias."

"Yes, but on a larger scale," Matias grinned.

"How large?" Ryan asked.

"Oh, nothing's decided yet," the man said. "We're just at the planning stage at the moment. But it's fairly obvious we need to switch to renewable energy sources as quickly as possible. The power people are considering a tidal barrage, maybe an offshore wind farm. Although there's no reason why we can't have both, and other energy generation methods, they do all work together. We're here to do the research. Well, we were."

The children all followed his gaze at the blackened mess that was once a warehouse.

"Did anything survive?" Conner asked.

"There might be something we can salvage, when we can have a proper look. But I'm not hopeful." The man shook his head. "Still, it will only delay things until we can replace what was lost. We'll be back."

"If you need anything, you can find us down at the harbor, in our boat, the 'eggy Su'. Just leave a note on the jetty if we aren't there."

The others smiled at the name and then nodded. "We certainly will. A small boat could be useful."

Matias laughed, "that's exactly what I said."

The children said their goodbyes and headed back to the 'eggy Su'. They talked as they approached the harbor, keeping their voices low.

"I think they're connected," Terry said. "Whoever cut the rope on Matias and Teuila's buoy also burned down the warehouse."

Conner nodded. "Agreed."

"Yep, got to be. Both renewable energy projects, both deliberate sabotage." Dawn added.

Jenna nodded. "This time last year I'd have said you were jumping to conclusions. After what we went through last summer, I'm going to say it's possible, but we need more evidence."

"Well," Ryan said smiling broadly, "looks like we've found this year's adventure!"

They were all in high spirits as they returned to the boat and set off for the BoatProf's island. They were looking forward to getting started, particularly since the whole thing had almost been cancelled when their parents found out about the academy.

"I can't believe our parents had a meeting about the BoatProf," Dawn said, "it's so embarrassing."

"I know," Conner agreed, "what were they thinking?"

"They could have just asked us," Ryan added. "It's not as if we're children anymore."

"Yeah, they called my parents as well," Terry said, "they started asking me questions when I got home, which was a surprise. I just told them the truth and they seemed happy enough."

"Wish I had your parents," Dawn said. "As you can imagine, my dad and stepmom went crazy. They were demanding answers, mostly from Ryan, which was actually hilarious." She smiled broadly.

"I'm glad you think it was funny," Ryan scowled.

"It was this time, I just sat there reading through my messages," Dawn said.

"And I like the way they decide we can go for one day to see how it goes," Ryan said angrily, "as if it's their decision!"

"My parents were actually saying they were going to come with me," Conner said in disbelief. "I'm glad I managed to talk them out of it."

"I'm just glad my gran knew the BoatProf," Jenna said. "I think it was her vouching for him that convinced them the prof was genuine."

"How does she know him, by the way?" Conner asked.

"She wouldn't say, she just smiled and said he was an old friend, one of a gang of people she used to hang out with."

"Oh, very mysterious."

"Yeah. It's funny how I don't think about her being young, but she obviously was once."

"Things were certainly different back then," Dawn said wisely.

"Gran says that a lot, about how much things have changed, but we still have a way to go."

"Exactly."

They got the journey time down to under ninety minutes, which was still quite a long time for a small boat on the open sea. As it was so far, they decided to spend whole days there, taking enough food and drink to last that long. Their first full day on the island would be spent with the prof teaching them how to read the plans for the old boat they were restoring, then, if time allowed, salvage as much of the old wreck as they could and transfer it to a dry building for reconstruction. Any parts of it that were unusable would be replaced, made by their own hands in the workshop.

As a side project, Ryan was gathering parts to use to convert 'eggy Su' into an electric boat. The BoatProf was very supportive of this move, but admitted it was a bit out of his area of expertise. Ryan had started watching online videos of people who'd done the same thing. He'd decided to ask Matias and Teuila if he got stuck on something.

Learning all the new terminology was a steep learning curve for the group. Every piece of wood, every joint, every tool seemed to have a name they were unfamiliar with. Occasionally, the Prof would throw in a word they did know, like transom or gunwale, and they would smile. Conner was particularly pleased when this happened, making sure the others knew he was responsible for that knowledge.

The old boat, it turned out, wasn't anywhere near as bad as they'd thought when it was buried in the mud. It was in hundreds of different pieces, but most of them just needed cleaning and reassembling. Despite the timber being treated, several parts were too rotten to use.

The professor led them over to his small wood store and opened the door. The children reacted to the odor immediately.

"Wow, that smells great!" Conner said.

The professor smiled. "I never get tired of it, no matter how many times I come in here."

He went over to some rough planks of wood and examined a few. "We could go with hackmatack, I've got plenty of that here, or white oak, although there might not be enough of that. Red oak? Ahh! I think we should go with this." He pulled out a small piece of wood and showed it to the children with a flourish. It was a rough brown colour and didn't look like much.

"From your expressions I can see you aren't impressed," he smiled. "But once this is cleaned up and treated it will take on a nice golden honey color, which should match well with what you already have. Anyone know what this is?"

"Oak?" Conner guessed.

"Oak is a hardwood, more durable but harder to work. This is cedar, grown on this very island. Technically a softwood, but perfect for boat building. The tree blew over in a storm a few years back, so I cut it up and it's been seasoning in here since then. Can't get much more local and sustainable than that!"

"Seasoning? Like salt and pepper?" Dawn asked.

"No, like curing. Fresh-cut timber is full of moisture and has to be dried before it's used. It causes all kinds of problems if you don't season it properly. We can look into how it's done later, as it's something I do regularly on the island. So, what do you think?" The professor presented the plank to the teens like he was trying to sell it to them.

They all agreed it was perfect, so they each grabbed a piece and took it back to the workshop to start their very first boat building project.

Some of the rotten pieces of the boat were complete but unusable. As these were the easiest parts to reproduce, the prof started them there. Each of the teens took a rotten piece of the boat and placed it on the new wood following the grain pattern, then drew around it with a pencil. This could then be cut out using the various hand and power-tools. The professor left them to it, but didn't go far in case they needed help.

Once they'd gotten past a certain point and knew what they were doing, they began to chat quietly among themselves.

"What we could do," Conner began, "is see if we can find other energy projects around here and stake them out, like we did with the dumpster and the ReKnew site last year."

Ryan nodded, "so we can catch the saboteurs red-handed when they turn up. Good plan."

"We need a phone signal for that," Dawn sighed.

"And I can ask my gran, she knows everybody in Stonehaven, apparently." Jenna laughed.

"Those people working for the power company, and Matias and Teuila, said they'd carry on with their projects," Terry said. "We already know them and where they are, so that's a good place to start."

"We need some cameras, those small ones the extreme sports people use. Then we can cover multiple targets," Ryan said.

"And where do we get those from and who's paying for them?" Dawn pointed out.

"Maybe we can get some second-hand ones, and we can all chip in."

Conner examined the piece of wood he was working on; it didn't really look like the original. "I think that might be a bit ambitious for us at this stage. Let's just stick to phones and eyes for now."

Ryan wasn't going to let it go so easily. "I'll still look into it. We might get lucky and pick some up really cheap."

"Aren't you supposed to be converting the boat?" Conner asked.

"Yes, I'm on it. Don't worry, we'll soon be slipping through the waves as silent as the wind." Ryan used his hand to illustrate the point.

"How are we going to charge the batteries if we convert it?" Jenna asked.

"I was thinking we could remove them and take it in turns to charge them at home overnight, until we can work something else out."

"Will that work?"

"Of course. Electricity is electricity, doesn't matter where it comes from."

"What about the different voltages?"

"There'd be a charger to sort all that out. One end plugs into the mains, the other goes into the battery pack."

"Ok, cool."

"And then we can really sneak around unnoticed," Dawn grinned, "not like that noisy, smoky old outboard we have now."

"We could ask the prof if we can put a charge-point here, in the harbor," Ryan suggested. "Hook it up to a wind turbine and we can charge all we want for free."

"He'll probably make us build it," Conner laughed.

"Great!" Ryan enthused, "I'm in!"

"Don't you have enough to do?" Terry pointed out, "Restoring this boat, cameras, electrifying the 'eggy Su' and now building a wind turbine."

"I like being busy."

Dawn tried to smother a laugh, mostly unsuccessfully. "What?"

Ryan glared at her but didn't reply.

They all returned to their tasks and slowly shaped the pieces they were each working on, with different levels of success. As it turned out, Terry was very good at woodworking. As both his parents were artists, and his dad carved beautiful wooden animals, perhaps it wasn't so surprising. Both Ryan and Dawn were competent, their work only needed a bit more work to make them just right. Jenna and Conner weren't so skilled. Terry had to finish Jenna's piece and Conner had to start again as he'd completely ruined his.

At the end of that first day of work they were all so tired they went home relatively early, much to the surprise of their parents. Although their minds were buzzing with new knowledge, they all fell asleep as soon as their heads hit the pillow.

CHAPTER FOUR

QUIET RUNNING

TO FATHOM

Originally, to fathom meant to check the depth of water under the ship. A fathom is the distance between the fingertips of a sailor's outstretched arms, standarized at six feet or 1.83 meters.

The meaning has now shifted to refer to someone solving a riddle or studying a certain subject in depth.

Luckily for the children, converting the boat to run on electricity was a lot easier, and cheaper, than they had guessed. Matias and Teuila had the idea of converting their existing outboard, which meant they could use the same propeller, the housing and the gearbox and still mount it in its usual place without drilling holes in the boat. They bought an old electric bicycle from a local second-hand store and used the motor and battery from that. Matias kindly donated the electronics and a second battery from an older design of their buoy, and it all worked perfectly, at least in the workshop.

Once it was fitted to the boat they had issues with the weight distribution, water getting in to the electrics, and the motor overheating. It was also a lot slower than the outboard and the batteries only gave them about 30 minutes of run time. Even so, the 'eggy Su' was much quieter, almost silent even at full revs, and there was no sign of any toxic fumes. So, they felt it worth persisting; and little by little they got the range and speed up, solved the overheating problem, and managed to find a balance between cooling and stopping sea spray getting inside. It wasn't perfect, more a work in progress, but it did everything they needed it to. Dawn in particular was delighted with how quiet it was.

Conner found the driving style and controls to be very similar, although he did find it accelerated faster and was overall easier to control the speed. Aside from the environmental benefits, and the sneak option, the biggest advantage to the teens was they were able to talk even when going at full speed. Today's main conversation was about another fire, this time on the edge of town.

"My gran said her friend could see a plume of black smoke rising from her yard," Jenna said.

"So it was nowhere near the other fire then," Dawn said, "it could still be linked though."

"We could check it out," Conner said, "but from what I saw online it was just a fire in an old house. The reporter said it was a derelict property, didn't even have a roof."

"Yeah, I saw that, and they blamed it on local youths, as usual," Ryan sighed.

"I can't see how it was linked to the energy stuff, but I think we should go and have a look, maybe just cycle past," Terry said.

"Maybe later, we have a job to do first," Conner pointed out, glancing down at the buoy sitting at his feet.

In return for Matias and Teuila's help with the boat, and because they were interested, the teens had agreed to deploy the experimental buoys for them. They had to be placed in relatively shallow water, sit just on the surface, and be out of the way of shipping and saboteurs. When checking out the BoatProf's island, they'd notice a sandbank they thought would be perfect. It was in sight of the island's harbor so they could keep an eye on it when they were there.

They were about halfway to their destination when Terry glanced over his shoulder and said, "someone's following us."

"What!" they all said, turning around.

"Don't all stare!" Terry hissed.

They turned and faced ahead, trying to act casual.

"What's happening, Terry?" Conner asked.

"There's a small cabin cruiser, sort of dirty brown. It was just out at sea when we left the harbor and now it's behind us."

"Are you sure it's following and not just going the same way?"

"It's matching our speed and staying parallel to our course, so I'm pretty sure. Turn east a bit, not too sudden."

A few minutes went by while Conner eased the tiller over and began to curve around to head east. More time passed, then Terry spoke again.

"Yes, it's changing course, staying parallel."

"What do we do now, there's not a lot of places to hide out here."

"If this was a car chase, we could slip down a side street and hide behind a truck or something," Ryan said.

"That helps," Dawn said sarcastically.

"Go faster," Terry suggested.

Conner twisted the throttle and the 'eggy Su' picked up speed. The batteries drained much faster at higher speeds so it wasn't something they could do for too long. He kept to the new easterly heading, planning to turn north and get back on course when they'd lost their pursuer.

Terry was concentrating hard, trying to listen. "They've sped up. Can you hear the engines? Twin fifties I think, overkill on that little boat."

"So we can't outrun it?"

"I doubt it. I think we need an upgrade."

"I've got my eye on a bigger motor," Ryan said happily. "It's twice the power, but we'll need bigger batteries as well."

"Doesn't help now though, does it?" Dawn snapped.

"Ok, calm yourself, Dant." Ryan used Dawn's childhood nickname because he knew it annoyed her.

Conner jumped in to stop the argument. "Can we keep the noise down? And does anyone have any ideas?"

"Stop here," Jenna suggested, "see what happens. But be ready to move again."

"Yes, grab the oars, pretend we're doing something here." Terry lifted one of the oars that were stowed along the sides of the boat and stood it upright.

Jenna did the same with the oar on her side and splashed around in the water. They could all hear the distant rumble of the outboards now, they sounded much smoother than their old engine.

"It's stopped, holding position," Terry said looking indirectly towards the other boat.

"Right, let's take a minute here," Conner spoke quietly as sound traveled very well over the open water. "We're thinking that whoever is in that boat is our saboteur, right?"

"Right." The others all agreed.

"So should we go over there and confront them, pretend we haven't noticed, or run for it?"

"I say we go over there and confront them, or at least get a photo, and maybe the name of the boat," Ryan suggested.

"I disagree," Dawn immediately replied.

"There's a surprise," Ryan mumbled.

Dawn carried on talking, looking at everyone but Ryan. "Remember last year? The person driving the boat wasn't the main criminal, that was Renzo Kneasley, right? Chances are this person is the same, not the top dog, just someone doing all the dangerous stuff."

"Yes, that's right," Conner nodded, "so we need to find out who this person is and see who they report to. Ok, stow the oars, we'll move off as if nothing's happened. Maybe they'll think we just deployed the buoy and then waste time looking for it while we get away."

Jenna looked at Terry, "would you recognize the boat again, if we found it later?"

"Yeah, I think so. That color is distinctive and a bit gross. And those engines will help me spot it."

Once the oars were stowed, and an extra few minutes later, Conner slowly accelerated away, continuing to head east and then gradually brought them back onto a northerly course. Terry kept watch for as long as he could. He turned to Dawn, "remember last year when you made a note to get binoculars? We should really get some." He grinned, making Dawn blush slightly.

Events played out exactly as they'd guessed. It looked like the small cruiser had headed straight over to their previous position as soon as they were far enough away. This distraction allowed them to escape and head for their real destination, as well as confirming whoever was in that boat was either the saboteur or linked to them.

Ryan, speaking mostly to Jenna, said, "well, there's no doubt now. Someone is up to something, damaging property and sabotaging equipment. I wonder how long that person has been following us, 'cause they were definitely waiting for us out there, Terry saw them."

"That's a scary thought," Jenna said. "And I wasn't doubting before, I was just saying we should make sure. Like we did last summer, we followed the whole chain from beginning to end before we told anyone."

"That worked very well," Conner sounded proud, "we need to do the same thing again. Dawn..." He was about to say she should be taking notes, but she'd already produced a fresh notebook and was writing down what they already knew.

"So we've got sabotage of equipment related to renewable energy... hmm, that word reminds me of someone, you don't think they'd be involved again, so soon after last year's narrow escape?"

"Who, Renzo and Regina? It's not impossible, some people never learn, and they did get away with it, for the most part," Conner replied. Dawn wrote 'R & R?' in her book, then on a new line wrote, 'dirty brown boat with big engines.'

"One thing's for sure," Terry said, "if we are being followed, we need to be careful of where we go and what we say in public places. Anyone could be the saboteur, so keep your eyes open."

"At least we're safe out here, and on the island," Jenna said.

"Do you think we should tell the BoatProf what's happening?" Conner asked. "We don't want to put him in danger."

"He already knows about the fire. And he knows what we're doing today, so I think he's aware," Jenna said.

Conner slowed the boat as they approached the sandbank. "Besides, I think the professor knows a lot more about things than we think."

With that enigmatic statement, Conner reached down and began preparing the buoy. It had to be activated using a magnet and the anchoring line had to be adjusted to approximately the right depth. Terry kept a lookout and reported the coast clear, there wasn't a single boat in sight, except those in the BoatProf's harbor, which was several hundred yards away.

The clear blue water revealed the rippled sandbank only four or five yards below the boat. Small fish darted over it and the occasional bubble or disturbance in the sand showed the presence of other sea creatures. With Terry on watch and Conner holding the boat steady against the current, Jenna and Ryan lowered the anchor, which was a large stone with a hole through it, until it hit the bottom. A quick adjustment was made and the buoy released. Dawn checked their exact position with the GPS on her phone and made a note of it. They checked it was working—the red LED flashing—and wasn't drifting, then headed towards the harbor to do more work on their new boat. Throughout the day, one of them stopped and looked towards the buoy's position. It was just a tiny red dot rising and falling with the swell, but they should easily be able to spot any boats approaching it.

Once again, Terry showed his skills, completing three quite complex pieces before the others had done one. Dawn and Ryan were able to make one each to the required standard. Jenna, with some help from Terry, finished her fairly simple piece later in the day. Conner decided his skills with wood weren't quite up to scratch, so he was given the task of sanding the finished pieces and keeping track of what was done and what wasn't.

As they worked, and during their frequent breaks, they tried to figure out what they needed to do to link the boat with the saboteur and then go up the chain of command to find the chief villain.

"Do we think this is just about renewable energy, like someone doesn't agree with it? Or is there more to it?" Conner asked.

"It's about money," Ryan said wisely. "It's always about money. What they say in the movies is 'follow the money'."

"What money?" Dawn said, "who's making money by burning down warehouses and cutting mooring lines?"

"Well, that's the question," Ryan grinned, "we find that out, we've cracked the case."

Conner looked doubtful. "I don't think it's that easy. And as Jenna has pointed out, we don't want to jump to conclusions. We need evidence, and we follow that until it leads to the saboteurs."

"Ok, so who would benefit, with money or anything else, if these projects were cancelled?" Terry asked.

"It can't be the power company, because they were affected," Dawn said.

"And it can't be an environmental group, because they'd support the projects," Jenna added.

Conner shook his head. "I'm confused. Maybe it is one person working alone, someone who hates renewable energy because of something that happened?"

"I bet you a 12" pizza with pineapple topping it's all about money," Ryan held his hand out.

Conner scowled at Ryan, "I'll bet you a 16" meat feast, but you know what you can do with the pineapple."

The others rolled their eyes as Ryan and Conner shook on the bet. It was something of an on-going joke between the pair and had stopped being funny to anyone else a long time ago.

"So," Dawn said to bring the conversation back on track, "the only clue we have so far is the dirty brown boat. The person or people on the boat cut the buoy loose, we're fairly sure of that, and possibly also set the warehouse on fire. We need to find the boat and whoever owns it."

Terry held up his hand to speak as if he was in school. He often did this and wasn't at all embarrassed about it. "There's definitely something more going on here. That warehouse had no sign on it, no one could have known what was in there just by looking. And that first buoy was at sea, the only way to have found it was by accident or by following Matias and Teuila when they put it there. How did the saboteur know they were going out to place a buoy in the first place?"

"In other words," Ryan pointed out, "the saboteur had information they shouldn't have had, which means other people are involved. See, I was right."

"We need to talk to Matias and Teuila again, see who else knew what they were doing and where they were going," Conner said. "And the same with the power company people, if they're still around."

"We could, but there's an obvious answer," Dawn said. "Who knows everything that happens in Stonehaven?"

Ryan laughed, "Jenna's gran!"

They all laughed at this, even Dawn.

"No, well, yes, but who else? Who knows because they're supposed to know, because they run the place?"

"The town council," Conner answered as they all nodded.

"Someone on the town council is giving, selling most likely, information to someone who's then either sabotaging the projects or paying someone to do it. The question is, why?"

"Money, that's why," Ryan insisted.

"But like we've already said, what money?" Conner asked.

"Another energy project maybe?" Dawn guessed.

"Are there other energy projects like these?" Jenna said.

"That's something else we need to find out," Conner said, "but I think finding that boat should be our main priority."

They all agreed to finish up what they were doing here and take a trip down the coast in the 'eggy Su' to check out the marina. They'd jury-rigged a stand and a power cable to allow them to remove the outboard and charge it while they worked. It meant removing and refitting the motor each time, but it was only meant to be a short-term solution until they could find a better one. By charging at both ends of their trips to the island, they were able to maintain more than enough range to safely reach either destination and still have power to spare.

After saying goodnight to the BoatProf and all the dogs, they boarded the boat and left. Bosun had been seen in the distance but not yet come close to the new arrivals. Conner steered them in close to shore until they had a phone signal and then each of them sent a text to their parents, telling them they were going to the marina to look at the boats and would be home later. They carried on south-west, passed the harbor and the beach, around the headland and then a short distance to Stonehaven Marina.

The contrast between the marina and the harbor was immediately obvious. Instead of dirty working boats with huge diesel engines, here they saw clean white yachts and cabin cruisers with fresh paint and chrome fittings. Each vessel had flags and colorful pennants flapping on the breeze. And there were actual people here, leaving, arriving, or just sitting on their decks drinking, chatting, laughing. And it didn't smell of fish, or exhaust fumes, or dead things floating in the water.

It wasn't often they came here, so the size and activity was a little shocking after the peace and quiet of the harbor and the island. The wooden jetties were built out from a stone quay like fingers, with boats moored bow first into each of the berths. They were arranged by size, the larger and more expensive vessels nearer to the entrance, getting smaller and cheaper, and less well-maintained, as they got further away.

Terry scanned the rows as Conner guided the boat slowly along the end of the jetties. They skipped the first few rows, which were large, expensive yachts; although none of them were super-yachts as seen in the more affluent resort towns. They couldn't just search up and down each jetty, that would be too obvious. They would just have to rely on Terry's keen eyes. By the time they'd ran out of marina to search, there was no sign of the brown boat.

"It would stand out against all the other shiny white and blue boats," Terry said, "I'm pretty confident it's not here."

"Wish we had a drone," Ryan said, "with a decent camera. We could search this place in minutes and not miss anything."

"Put it on the list of things we don't have," Conner complained.

"Where else could it be?" Jenna asked.

"Must be on one of the islands," Dawn guessed.

Conner turned the 'eggy Su' and headed back to the harbor. "It will take us a long time to look on every island and some of them have boat-houses, so we might miss it anyway."

"There's only one thing left to do then," Terry said, "wait for them to reappear and follow them home."

CHAPTER FIVE

BUOYS AND COOKIES

IN THE OFFING

The Offing is the part of the sea visible from shore but too far out for a ship to moor or reach an anchoring point. A ship might stay in the offing if it's too dangerous to come closer to shore, during a storm for instance.

It's modern meaning is of an event or result that will almost certainly happen in the very near future.

A familiar sight greeted them a few days later when they reached the harbor to go to the island. In the berth previously occupied by the Sea Fox, a ship was moored. It was clean and shiny, with a new paint job, rigged up with solar panels. The deck was clear and the navigation equipment was all new and fully working. The teens were puzzled to see the ship was called 'Sea Fox III'.

Ryan stood staring at it, "that can't be Marty's old trawler. It never looked like that when he owned it."

"No, but that's definitely it. It was sold at auction, so these people must have bought it." Conner looked closer at the people who had appeared from below deck. "Isn't that the man from the power company, the one Matias was talking to?"

"Looks like him," Ryan agreed.

Jenna stood and climbed out of the boat. "Let's go and talk to them." She walked off, closely followed by Dawn and then the boys. They all walked around the quay and soon arrived at the Sea Fox's berth. They stood waiting to be seen, which didn't take long.

The man smiled when he recognised them and walked over to the gunwale. "Hello, so this is where you hang out."

"This is our home base," Jenna replied, "but we move around a lot."

"Very good. Do you like our new research vessel?"

"It's great," Ryan beamed.

"Glad you like it. It's fully electric, solar powered, and much more secure than the old warehouse. I'd invite you aboard but we have some items that have to stay confidential, for now."

"Ok, sure."

"Did you know the previous owner?"

"Yes, we saved his life," Dawn said.

"Wow, that's great. I'd love to hear about it when I have more time. I have to get back to work now, we're still installing our equipment. I'm Aksel, by the way. Let me know if you need anything."

"A solar panel," Ryan called out.

Aksel laughed, "I'll see what I can do."

The teens said their goodbyes and headed back to their boat, pushing Ryan along in front of them.

"Why did you shout 'solar panel' at him? you're so embarrassing," Dawn demanded when they were out of ear shot.

"It's to charge the boat, we can set it up as a roof and then we won't need to keep taking the motor off. And you're embarrassing," Ryan retorted.

"It's a good idea," Conner admitted, "but I don't think it was appropriate to be asking someone we barely know for one."

They all stopped talking as they noticed Terry had spotted something. Anyone who didn't know him as well as they did wouldn't have seen any change. He was acting like any other teen, looking at his phone.

They all sat down and tried to be casual, taking out their own phones, or in Conner's case, the old book of maritime knowledge. They were all silent for a while as they let Terry do his thing.

He finally spoke, using Abenaki-Penobscot so they knew it was serious. "Behanem. Pazobimuk pados."

A woman was watching the ship. Conner hadn't seen anyone so he asked where she was. "Toni?" he asked.

"Pasojiwi paskakan."

Conner stretched and looked indirectly towards the harbor entrance; there was no one there.

"Was it someone you know?" Conner whispered, his Abenaki-Penobscot not good enough yet.

"Pilwaka."

A stranger, although they didn't know everyone in town so it could still have been a local.

"Nosoka Behanem?" Dawn asked if they should follow her.

"I'll go and have a wander around the parking lot, see if she's out there," Terry said. "You lot wait here; we don't want to spook her."

He returned several minutes later and climbed back into his seat. "I saw her again but she's very cautious and she soon took off. I think she's more interested in the Sea Fox than us, she was watching some of the crew unloading supplies from a van."

"What did she look like?" Conner asked.

"She was taller than Ryan, about five eight or nine, her hair was dark red and had a rough texture, like it had been dyed too many times. I didn't get a good look at her face, so I didn't see anything distinctive. She was wearing old blue jeans and a blue quilted jacket with a raised collar. She seemed... not an expert but like she'd done this before."

"I'd say we've found our saboteur, or at least one of them," Conner said.

The teens carried on with their routine for the next several days, going to the island and working on the boat, learning new skills from the professor and generally being teenagers. As already arranged with Matias and Teuila, when they left the island that evening, they picked up the buoy they'd deployed earlier and headed back to the harbor. The little red LED was still winking inside the plastic box to show it was still on. It would have collected a lot of data while it was in the sea, and Matias and Teuila would be eager to see the results.

The teens had found an old blanket to wrap the buoy in to hide it from prying eyes. They weren't sure this was strictly necessary as the saboteur seemed to know their every move, but they didn't want to make it easy for them. Sure enough, as they headed for the workshop on Mason Road Terry, who was slightly behind the others, whispered a warning. "Pilwaka."

The teens kept walking, Jenna and Ryan carrying the blanket, Conner slightly ahead with Dawn.

"Toni?" Conner asked quietly.

"Odaoak punjiwi."

So she was behind them, had probably followed them from the harbor. "She probably knows where we're going, but I still think we should try and lose her," Conner whispered, "I don't like being followed."

"Me neither," Dawn agreed, "but then she'll know we've seen her."

"Can we lose her without her knowing, just turn a corner and hide somewhere?" Ryan asked.

"I know a place we can hide, if we can get there before she sees us," Terry said.

"Where?"

"The burned out warehouse. It looked like there was a small office at the back, we could hide in there."

"Is it safe to go inside? The whole front wall is missing," Jenna asked.

"If it hasn't fallen down yet, I don't think it will," Ryan said.

"Ok, let's have a look at least," Conner suggested, "If it doesn't look safe, we'll just carry on."

With the plan agreed, Terry began to hang back a few paces, pretending to be engrossed in something on his phone. Sure enough, the woman slowed to keep pace. The others turned the next corner and ran along the street, turning another and heading for the warehouse. Luckily, the buoy wasn't heavy; they'd left the anchor stone in the 'eggy Su' ready for the next deployment. The burned building was still standing as solid as ever, cordoned off with tape and a few wooden pallets. The smell wasn't as strong but still irritated their nostrils as they got closer. Conner lifted the tape at a suitable point and Jenna and Ryan ran inside, quickly followed by Dawn and then Conner.

There were a few small rooms at the rear of the warehouse, opposite the missing wall. One of them was a rest room, so they headed for the next one, a small office with windows looking out onto the warehouse. They slipped inside and shut the door, putting the buoy on the ground. Jenna pulled out a corner of the blanket and she and Dawn sat on it. The boys just sat on the floor. Their heads were just below the level of the glass. By rising up a little Ryan could keep watch through the gaping hole and into the street beyond. The smell of smoke was still strong in here, but was made worse by a damp odour like a wet toilet.

The teens kept as silent as they could as they waited. Time passed, the smells began to irritate their noses and the hard floor became increasingly uncomfortable. They began to hear faint noises as the silence continued; the ticks and creaks of the metal building as it cooled after a day in the sun. At least, that's what they hoped it was, and not something more sinister. A loud buzzing suddenly filled the small space, making them all jump.

Dawn pulled her phone out. "It's from Terry, he says 'Alosa'." Dawn smiled despite the situation. "Go."

Conner stood and slowly opened the door. After a quick look around, he gestured for them to follow. Jenna and Ryan grabbed the bundle and headed out, Dawn close behind, closing the office door as she left.

Back on the street, the four headed straight for Matias and Teuila's place as quickly as they could. As the teens had contacted the scientists when they reached the harbor, they were both waiting for them and ushered them into their workshop and closed the door.

"Everything ok?" Matias asked.

"We were followed," Conner explained, "Terry's led her away somewhere, he should be here soon."

"Will he be ok?" Teuila sounded worried.

Ryan shrugged, "yeah, he loves this kind of thing."

"Did you see who was following you?" Matias asked.

"Terry did, said it was a woman with dark red hair, he'd never seen her before."

"I'd like to know how she found out what we were doing," Matias said.

"We have a theory about that," Conner offered.

"Yes?"

"It's someone on the town council, got to be," Jenna said.

"Hmm, makes sense."

Dawn opened the door slightly. "Terry's here."

The young man walked silently into the workshop, a grin on his face. "That was fun."

"What happened?" Dawn asked.

"I led her in a circle back to the harbor. At every corner I shouted, 'wait up guys!' and pretended I was busy with my phone. Here, I got video."

They all moved in closer as Terry showed them a video he'd taken with his phone. He was walking at the time, recording over his shoulder, so it wasn't great, but it gave them all a good look at the woman. No one recognized her, but at least they now knew what she looked like.

"Good job everyone!" Matias said.

"Yes, very good!" Teuila gave them all a bright smile.

The boys blushed slightly at her praise, looking anywhere but at her.

Matias saved them. "Right, let's get this thing open and see what we've got."

The teens helped the couple dismantle the assemblage and separate out the electronics from the other parts. The buoy and the other sections were stowed neatly in their proper place, much to Jenna's pleasure, and the electronics were soon exposed and connected to an ancient laptop. Matias began tapping and clicking away and after a few minutes stood back.

He smiled, "it looks like we got some good data, or at least plenty of it. Might take a while to upload on this old laptop, let's go inside and get you all some milk and cookies."

Teuila laughed, "they aren't little children."

"So, beer then?"

"Stop teasing them. We have coffee, tea, soda, or water, if you prefer."

"But we can still have cookies, right?" Matias asked.

"Yes."

They all piled into the tiny cottage kitchen and squashed themselves onto short benches at a small table. They were all given drinks, and a large plate of cookies was placed in the center of the table. It soon became obvious none of them were too old for cookies, as they all disappeared very quickly.

The conversation soon turned to their saboteur and then to the events of the previous summer. In this area, it seemed the teens had far more experience of such things than the adults, who listened to their theories with interest.

When those topics were exhausted, Matias and Teuila filled them in on their own backgrounds. Both of them were born in the US, as were their parents. Matias' grandparents were originally from Chile, and Teuila's ancestors were Polynesian, mostly Samoan. They'd met at university and each found a kindred spirit in the other. Their plan, as they described it, was to revolutionize electricity generation, and set it free from big business.

They finally said their goodbyes as the light began to fade. The teens headed home and the scientists went to analyse their data. Dawn was itching to get involved with that, but it had to stay confidential for the moment. Terry went out first to scout around, although they were pretty sure the woman with red hair already knew where Matias and Teuila lived. The scientists gave them a sort of watered-down parental lecture on keeping safe and not doing anything silly, which the teens nodded along to, and promised to contact the authorities as soon as they had any information.

Naturally, the whole staying safe thing was forgotten by the next morning when they all gathered in the harbor.

"So," Conner began, taking his usual seat at the tiller, "what's our next move?"

"We have an image of our saboteur, let's see if we can find her." Terry sent the video to all their phones and the hunt began.

The next few hours or so passed without success. It soon became obvious, by the sound of gunfire coming from his phone, that Terry had given up for the moment. This was quickly followed by Jenna enthusing about racing bikes and Dawn explaining where the word 'sabotage' came from, which had nothing to do with throwing sandals into machines like a lot of people thought. It soon became apparent Ryan had fallen asleep, and Conner was reading his maritime book.

They all decided, when they were all awake and paying attention, that it was unusual for anyone not to have some kind of online presence, but not impossible. Their last chance was for Jenna to show the video to her gran and hope she could help.

Jenna took a still from the video and sent it to her gran. It was the best image they could find of her face in the whole thing, they just had to hope it was good enough. While they waited for a reply, Conner began to ask them questions from his book.

"The series of lines and markings on a ship to indicate a safe load in different seas is called: A, the sneaker line, B, the Wellington line, or C, the Plimsoll line?"

"Give us the answers again," Ryan said.

Conner repeated the question.

"I don't think it's sneaker, sounds too modern, I'm going with B," Dawn guessed.

"I'll say A," Ryan said.

"I'll take C, then at least one of us is right," Jenna answered.

"Terry?" Conner prompted.

"Yeah, B, sounds right."

"And the answer is… they're named after the British MP Samuel Plimsoll who championed their use in the 1860s. One point to Jenna."

"So the shoes were named after a person?" Ryan asked, "like Wellington boots."

There was some tapping from Dawn's direction, "No, plimsoll shoes are named after the Plimsoll mark because of the line on the side of the shoe."

"So they were then. The line was named after a person and the shoe was named after the line. Same thing really." Ryan insisted.

"No, there's an extra step. You can't just ignore it," Dawn said with rising annoyance.

Conner was just about to ask another question to defuse the tension when Jenna's phone vibrated.

"It's from gran, let's see. 'hi sweetie cant b sure but looks like Amelia Stackpole but shed…' "oh, 'she'd', wish gran would learn to type punctuation, 'be older now take care gran kiss'."

Furious typing followed until Dawn shouted, "gotcha!"

"You found something, Dawn?" Conner asked casually.

"Oh yes, and… oh damn! Wow, saw that coming. Wait, what?"

The others waited impatiently until Dawn noticed them glaring.

"Amelia Stackpole runs a printing company with her two daughters, Virginia and Verbena. That's an older post. New post, Amelia Stackpole runs a printing company with her daughter, Virginia. What's happened to Verbena?"

"Are you going to tell us?" Conner asked.

"'Verbena Stackpole, navy veteran, sentenced to five years in prison for theft and assault of multiple persons'. So she must have been released recently."

"Wow, that's..."

"There's more. Guess who Amelia Stackpole has a picture of, tagged 'me and my cousins'?"

"Someone we know?" Conner asked, "a local?"

"Oh yes."

"The Kneasleys?" Jenna guessed.

"Correct!"

"What're those old rogues up to these days?" Ryan said.

"Nothing new, at least according to the ReKnew website." Dawn scanned the business page but nothing had really changed. "And being cousins doesn't prove they are working together or even like each other."

"They don't have to like each other to work together," Ryan pointed out, "and I'd say if something's going down in this town Renzo and Regina are behind it."

"What we need is a contact on the local council, just like the saboteurs have," Jenna said, "I wonder if my gran knows anyone?"

"You know," Dawn pointed out, "some stuff is available for the public to look at, planning decisions and such things. It's not all secret. Some of it might even be online, public consultations and things like that."

"Ok, do you want to look into that? I have to work later," Conner said. He helped his parents in their pizzeria some evenings, mainly doing menial tasks in the kitchen like slicing meat and cleaning up.

Dawn smiled, "of course."

They spent the rest of the day on a slow tour of the area, going up as far as Moon Crescent Beach and down to the marina. They kept an eye open for the brown boat as they talked, ate their lunch and dozed in the the sun, but didn't see it or anything else suspicious. At one point they turned off the motor and let the 'eggy Su' drift on the slow current.

The gentle motion and the familiar sounds of the sea eased their minds and bodies. In later life, they would look back on moments like this, and realise just how lucky they were.

DECOYS AND DISTRACTIONS

LEEWAY

The amount of drift experienced by a ship caused by the wind blowing against it is called Leeway. The motion of the ship is leeward, which is the direction the wind is going, as opposed to windward, which is where the wind is coming from.

In modern times, it's come to mean a certain amount of flexibility given in certain situations. This could be time, space, or even materials.

A few days later, the teens were away from the sea for a change. Dawn had searched the local council's website and found an application for the installation of a solar farm, which immediately caught her attention. There was no name given on the public version, only a location. By talking to her dad and stepmom, who were realtors, she'd also found a piece of land for sale by auction, although a rival company were handling the sale. She didn't think the two pieces of information were related until she saw the small map included with the article. When she double checked, it seemed the fire that had destroyed the old house was in that same field. The teens hadn't investigated it further because it was inland and they didn't see a link between the field and the renewable energy projects.

It was another warm day with only a soft breeze moving the tops of the trees. The teens had walked up the hill from Terry's house on the edge of town. They kept out of sight as much as possible, although they were doing nothing wrong. The roads narrowed as they moved out of the suburbs and into the rural area. The amount of traffic reduced to almost nothing, allowing the sound of bird song and trilling insects to be heard. Low hills rose up beyond the town, covered in trees and dotted with small buildings. This far above Stonehaven, they could see the town was surrounded by soft green countryside. It was very picturesque, but mostly wasted on the young teens.

To them, everything was different here; the countryside smelled wrong, the light had a different quality and the sound of the waves was missing. Looking back, they could see the ocean, blue and calm under the bright sun. Boats headed out to sea from the marina and large container ships could be seen crossing the horizon. They all wanted to be back down there, but they had something else to do today.

They'd almost missed the event, but the five of them had arrived just as several other interested parties had turned up in expensive-looking cars. The owners parked their shiny black limos or red sports models on the narrow road, blocking it completely for anything larger than a bicycle.

The people who got out of them were dressed as if they were going to a fancy event. There were several comments about the mud, particularly in regard to its effect on expensive shoes. The teens were surprised to see quite a crowd gathering. Each car had multiple occupants, as if it was some kind of family outing to the countryside.

In contrast to every other field in the area, this one was surrounded only by a simple wire fence. The lack of trees and undergrowth left the teens a little exposed as they approached the busy entrance. They managed to find a few low bushes as they made their final approach, waiting there until everyone had gotten out of their vehicles and gone into the field. It wasn't particularly large as fields went, although none of them had much experience of such things. The promotional material for the sale said it was 4.4 acres, although this didn't help them a lot either. In the end they decided it was about 4 or 5 football fields. The property had actually been up for sale for some time. The realtor's website showed a picture of the house before the fire. It looked solid, but the doors and windows had been vandalized and the front wall was covered in graffiti. It was easy to see why the press had instantly assumed the fire was started by teens.

At the moment, the field was covered in sparse, newly-mown grass, apart from one end where the house had stood. What had once been someone's home had either been demolished or had collapsed, the burnt timbers forming a somber pile at the end of a pitted gravel drive. A large area around the house was scorched black, including the grass and a few trees, only their stumps remaining. What might have been a car or tractor was reduced to a lump of melted metal. There was a distinct smell of farm animals on the air, smothered by the smell of ash when the wind changed direction.

Jenna's gran had told her the field had once been part of a large farm, but the owners had sold it off bit by bit to pay off debts incurred after the failure of several get-rich-quick schemes. The house had been abandoned at some point and slowly fell into disrepair. Even at that stage, the house could have been fixed up and used as a home by someone.

Dawn had discovered there were very complicated laws about what you could and couldn't do on a piece of land, with the final decision made by the council. As this was rural land, no one was allowed to build anything more than a few houses on it or use it for raising crops or livestock or similar activities. There were a few exceptions; as renewable energy was in the spotlight at the moment, covering the field in solar panels was apparently ok. Provided, of course, it wasn't suitable for occupation. Someone had made sure that was no longer the case.

The auction was held in the actual field, the participants making use of the driveway as much as possible to keep their nice shoes clean. With the auctioneer standing on a box and the potential buyers gathered around in a semi-circle, the event started. Directly in the centre stood Renzo and Regina Kneasley, bidding loudly as if they could win the auction by making the most noise. The teens didn't know if the couple knew what they looked like; their names hadn't been published after last year's adventure and certainly not their photos. But the couple weren't above paying someone to find out. They kept their distance just in case, letting Terry get closer to confirm it was them and if they bought the land.

There was no question of course, and soon the Kneasleys were shaking hands with the realtor and what they assumed was the land owner as the rest of the bidders returned to their vehicles. Just in case, Dawn made a note of all the registration plates in case they turned up again later. The teens let the crowds disperse and return to their busy days and then headed back to the harbor.

"They took a bit of a risk," Conner said as they walked back towards Stonehaven, "the Kneasleys; if they applied for planning permission before they'd even bought the land."

"It seems to me they were confident they would win, maybe they faked the whole thing. Hired some people to pretend to bid and then drop out," Dawn said.

"I wouldn't be surprised," Ryan sighed.

"I'm beginning to think this contact they have on the council isn't just giving them information," Jenna said, "it looks like they're doing them favors as well."

Conner nodded, "looks like it. They paid red hair to burn down the house so they could get the land cheaper, probably, and then paid the council person to make sure the planning permission was going to go through before they bought the field."

"Looks that way," Terry agreed, "but what are we going to do? A solar farm would be a great thing to have in this area, but we don't want the Kneasleys in charge of it."

"We don't. And as Aksel said, we can have more than one renewable energy project." Conner said.

"It actually says that on the council website, that they're allowing one renewable energy project this year, as a trial run for future projects. So the Kneasleys are trying to make sure theirs is the only one, probably to make more money," Dawn said.

"Told you," Ryan grinned, "it's always about money."

"And, of course," Conner said, somewhat angrily, "they got old red hair to sabotage the other projects so none of them would be ready by the deadline, so the council member can honestly say there was only one choice, whoever they are."

"It'll be the mayor," Ryan laughed, "they say that in crime movies all the time, 'this thing goes right to the top!'"

"We still need proof of all this," Jenna pointed out. "Remember last year, how we followed the whole chain? I think this is more of a web, but we still need to do the same thing."

"Where do we start?" Conner asked.

Terry smiled, "let's set a trap for the saboteur."

The next day the teens visited Matias and Teuila's workshop to pick up two items. One of them was the buoy they'd previously deployed, the other, which looked exactly the same, was a decoy. They carried both of the buoys wrapped in the same blanket so the saboteur wouldn't notice. The group suspected she'd be waiting for them out to sea. After a conversation with the scientists, it turned out they had to get official permission to deploy the buoys in the sea, which answered the question of how the saboteur found out. Almost any council employee could get access to the paperwork.

Conner guided the 'eggy Su' out of the harbor entrance and headed up the coast towards Crescent Moon Beach at about half speed. Sure enough, Terry soon spotted the dirty brown boat a short distance away, a red-haired figure was sitting on deck with a fishing rod in their hands. After a few minutes, the fishing rod was stowed and the boat began to move on a parallel course in the same direction. The roar of the cabin cruiser's twin outboards was clearly audible and in stark contrast to the almost silent electric motor moving the 'eggy Su'.

When they found a suitable spot for the decoy buoy, they continued with the charade of setting it in the right place and making a note of the GPS coordinates. It had to look genuine and take the same amount of time or the woman would become suspicious. They anchored it in almost the same spot as the original, on a sandbank just off the beach. When that was done, they headed off towards the BoatProf's island, aiming to place the actual buoy on the seaward side this time. It would be out of sight of the island's harbor, but they were the only ones who knew where it was. Once this was done, Conner guided the 'eggy Su' into the harbor and everyone went ashore. All they could do now was wait for part two of their plan to work out.

The professor was there as usual and was introduced to Matias and Teuila, who had taken Ryan and Jenna's places on the boat to make up the numbers. Meanwhile, Ryan and Jenna were waiting out to sea in the scientists' kayaks ready to follow the dirty brown boat back to wherever it moored. Because their cell-phones didn't work out here, they wouldn't know if the pair were successful until they returned later.

Matias and Teuila were immediately impressed by the BoatProf and his academy. They were given a tour of the facility, were mobbed by the dogs, and even Bosun put in an appearance, taking an immediate liking to Teuila. They generally thought it was a great idea. The professor tried to recruit the pair, but they said they were far too busy at the moment. They did promise to return as soon as they had time. The teens showed them their boat, or at least the parts they'd made as none of them were actually connected to any other at the moment. They seemed impressed, and asked the teens to make one for them, which would be an improvement on their kayaks.

The day wore on and there was no sign of Ryan and Jenna. The others decided to leave early and see what had happened to them. The scientists also wanted to return to their work, so they said their goodbyes to the professor and headed home. Conner let them each take a turn with the 'eggy Su' during the journey. Both were impressed with the smooth and quiet ride and the quick acceleration.

The two orange kayaks were pulled up onto the jetty when they entered the harbor. Ryan and Jenna were sitting there with them, looking wet and disheartened.

"We lost her," Jenna admitted when the 'eggy Su' pulled into its berth. "She sped by us on those two engines she's got and we couldn't paddle fast enough."

"Yeah, she was too fast and we weren't close enough to see where she went," Ryan said, "We should have gone closer but we didn't want to be spotted. I'm fairly sure she didn't see us, or didn't know who we were if she did."

"We tried to follow the wake those engines made, but we aren't great at tracking, we should have taken Terry," Jenna admitted.

"But I can't kayak, and they're single-seaters," Terry said. "Besides, you were probably too low in the water to get a good view of the wake."

"Did you get an approximate position?" Teuila asked.

"Well," Ryan said, "somewhere between south of the beach headland and north of the marina. She seemed to just turn in towards the shore at some point. I think she shut off one of the outboards because it went a lot quieter and the wake faded away."

"There aren't any mooring spots along there," Dawn said, scrolling through a map on her phone, "as far as I can see. The coastal path runs along the hill above, and the trees grow almost down to the sea all along there."

Ryan looked over dawn's shoulder and pointed, "look at all these inlets and coves, she must be mooring up in one of those. She's going to take some finding."

"That's how it goes sometimes," Terry reassured them. "It can take a while to find someone who doesn't want to be found, and she's a navy veteran. At least we've narrowed it down."

"So we need to do it again, but be waiting along that stretch of coastline next time," Conner said.

"Right," Ryan said, "how long do we have to teach Terry to Kayak?"

They all laughed but agreed it would be a good idea. Kayaking in the sea wasn't an easy skill to learn, and they all thought it would take more time than they had for him to be competent and safe. With that decided, they all helped Matias and Teuila to load their kayaks onto their car and then went their separate ways.

Back in the 'eggy Su', they all gathered around Ryan as he showed them where he thought they'd lost the saboteur on a map on his phone. Jenna added her opinion and they soon settled on an approximation of where she was hiding the boat and where they could start their search.

"I suppose it might be better to hike along the trail instead of using the boat," Conner said, "might be less obvious what we're doing."

"Just because she's mooring there doesn't mean she's living on her boat," Jenna pointed out. "She could be leaving it there and then going somewhere else."

"Good point," Conner said, "but then she'd need to get in and out, and the footpath is the only way to do that."

Dawn studied the map. "There're no buildings out there, so if she's living in town that's a good distance away. And that trail isn't wide enough for anything more than a horse, so she can't be driving."

"What about a motorcycle?" Ryan suggested. "She seems to like loud engines."

Dawn nodded. "Possible I suppose, but it would be a bit obvious, and vehicles aren't allowed on the coastal trail."

"They aren't allowed on Moon Crescent either, but that didn't stop them last year," Ryan said.

"True." Dawn agreed.

"Maybe we could stake out the trail," Ryan looked at Terry, "whatever she's using we could follow her back to the boat, be much easier to find it that way."

"That won't work if she is living on the boat. It might be better to let her come to us," Terry said, "like we did today. It could take days to find her and it's never a good idea to corner someone, they tend to get nasty."

"Yeah, maybe." Conner agreed. "And everyone is aware she's out there now, and are taking precautions so there's no real urgency."

"Or maybe she'll make a mistake and get caught," Dawn said.

Terry shook his head. "She doesn't seem the type to mess up. I bet she spends hours on that boat planning everything to the last detail."

"So, if we can get on the boat, we could find all the evidence!" Dawn smiled.

"Good idea. We need the boat as well as Verbena."

"Ok," Conner said as they prepared to head home, "we agree we need to find both of them, although if we find just the boat, we can leave the rest to the police."

"We could split up," Ryan suggested. "Have some of us in the boat and some on land, keep a parallel course until we find her. If we don't go too far out, we can communicate by phone."

"Not sure I like that plan, but we might not have a choice," Conner said.

"Why don't we just think about it for a while?" Dawn suggested.

"Sounds good."

CHAPTER SEVEN

VISIT FROM THE SEA

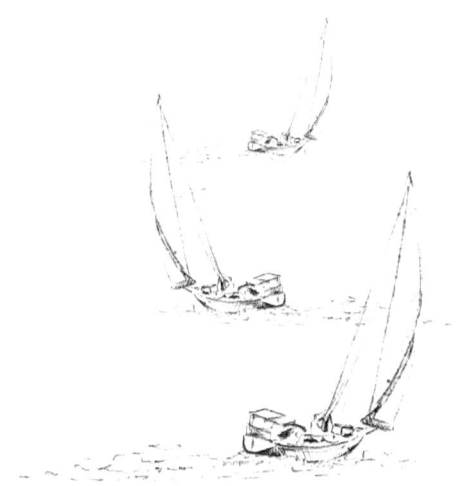

CHANGING TACK

Sailing ships can't travel directly into the wind. If a ship needs to go in that direction, a series of changes in heading, or tacking, allows the ship to zigzag and follow the approximate course required.

The modern meaning is much wider and more diverse, generally referring to trying new ideas, methods or ways of doing things to try and solve a problem.

The teens spent the next several days working on their boat on the BoatProf's island. It was slow going, but they were getting faster as they grew in confidence and skill. There would soon be enough parts to begin assembly. They had all decided to name the boat only when it was complete, just before they launched it. As they were making it almost from scratch, they could add an electric motor and batteries into the design, instead of adding them after, like they had with the 'eggy Su'. The main propulsion would be provided by the sails, and as none of them were experienced sailors, this was another set of skills they'd need to learn.

They talked as they worked, of course, mostly about what they were doing, but also about how they could get internet access on the island. As they were out of cell-phone range they weren't able to keep up with the local news or research any of their theories on the whole sabotage thing. This usually meant they spent their evenings ashore doing their searches, and then talked about it on their way to Rogue Island in the 'eggy Su'.

This morning it was warm but the wind had picked up, blowing along the coast and raising a choppy sea. The wind blew into their faces as they headed north towards the island, causing Conner to compensate by turning the throttle more and so using more battery power. They, with the prof's help, had set up a charging point of sorts near the harbor. They'd found some designs online and made a wind turbine, which they had mounted on a broken mast standing upright on the highest point above the harbor. A long cable ran down to the boat to allow them to connect up without removing the motor every time. It was crude and inefficient, but it worked, as long as there was a decent wind, which was most of the time out here.

It was Jenna who had the most interesting news this morning. "My gran says the Kneasleys are having a party on Saturday, on a huge, fancy yacht she says. Strictly invitation only. All of Stonehaven's rich and powerful have been invited, apparently."

"Did she say what they're celebrating?" Conner asked.

"No, it's probably just rich folk bragging about how much money they have."

"Does she know where the yacht is going to be?" Dawn asked.

"They're starting in the marina but the invites mention some kind of moonlight cruise, weather permitting."

"I bet we could see some interesting stuff on that yacht," Dawn said, "like who the Kneasleys are hanging out with."

"Like council members," Ryan said, "but how do we get aboard?"

"We don't need to get on the yacht, just take pictures of the people as they get on and off." Terry said. "And as most yachts only have one gang plank, we know exactly where they'll be."

Dawn smiled. "Yes, good point. We need to be fairly close though, to get good pictures."

"From what I remember, the jetties in the marina are only open to owners," Conner said, "and I'll bet the Kneasleys have extra security. We won't get near that ship."

"So what do we do?" Ryan asked.

"Does anyone have a camera, you know, a real one?" Jenna held up her phone, "not one of these. One with a huge lens so we can watch without going into the marina."

They all shook their heads.

"We might be able to get some powerful binoculars," Dawn said, "but that won't really help."

"No, we need to take photos to use as evidence," Ryan said.

"Well, there's only one way to do it then," Terry said, "we'll have to follow the yacht out to sea and take pictures as best we can, using what we have. The sea isn't anyone's property, so we can go wherever we want."

"These modern yachts have huge windows anyway," Ryan pointed out, "so we should be able to get some decent shots with our phones. But what if they go below deck?"

"Selfie sticks!" Dawn said loudly. "We can lift them up and look through the portholes, take videos and then edit out the best bits."

Conner smiled at Dawn. "You really are getting sneaky; Terry is a bad influence."

Dawn blushed slightly and looked away.

Terry was about to reply, then stopped and looked down. "There's a lot of water in here. It didn't rain last night."

They all looked down, Jenna lifting her feet off the bottom to keep her shoes dry. "Is it getting deeper?"

"Looks like it, I think we have a leak." Terry knelt down and began to examine the hull under his seat. "Looks like the hull's split. Every time we go over a wave more water comes in."

Conner slowed the boat a little. "We need to start bailing, use whatever you have."

Ryan leaned down and tried to scoop the water up with his hands. He didn't get much.

Jenna pulled a cotton t-shirt out of her bag. "I hope you all appreciate this." She dropped the shirt into the water, let it soak some of it up, and then wrung it out over the side. "Well, that's ruined."

"I think it's getting deeper faster; the hull is splitting more." Terry grabbed a discarded pizza box that was now floating in the bottom of the boat. By using it as a scoop he managed to stop the water rising a little, but it was still coming in and the pizza box was losing its strength the wetter it got.

There was at least a couple of inches of water in the boat now. The situation had gone bad very quickly. Dawn grabbed a plastic bottle from her bag and quickly drank the water. She then filled the bottle with sea water and tipped it over the side. Despite their combined efforts, the water was still rising and the boat was rapidly getting lower in the water. Soon, the waves would be coming over the sides and into the boat, which would short out the batteries and leave them without power.

Conner watched Dawn bailing and then had an idea. He pulled out his own water bottle, drank most of the contents, then replaced the cap. With his penknife he cut the end off the bottle, then made another U-shaped cut from that to form a crude scoop. "Dawn, try this."

Dawn looked over and grabbed the scoop, passing her own bottle to Conner. "Make another one."

Conner set to work converting Dawn's bottle. "Anyone else got a plastic bottle?"

It turned out they all did. Conner took them one by one and cut them to shape. Soon they were all bailing as fast as they could go and much more efficiently. They succeeded in stopping the water level rising, even reduced it a little, but it was still coming in. Conner twisted the throttle as far as he dared. A glance ahead showed him they were in sight of the BoatProf's island, although at this point it was just a dark shape on the horizon. They needed to keep going a little longer and they'd all be safe.

Now they all had scoops, Jenna tried to use the ruined t-shirt to bung up the hole. It worked for a while, but the split just kept growing. The teens all bailed as fast as they could, reducing the water level a good few inches; but they were soon out of breath.

"Dawn, swap with me for a while, take a break." Conner said.

Without a word, Dawn moved over to the rudder and passed her scoop to Conner, who took her place and began bailing furiously, as if he was personally responsible for the situation. The island crept closer but they were barely winning the battle with the cold sea as they grew hotter and began to exhaust themselves.

"The boat won't sink," Conner said to reassure them, and himself. "And we're wearing lifejackets. If the engine cuts out, we'll have to use the oars. Me and Ryan can row, Terry and Jenna can bail, Dawn can keep us heading towards the island. We can swap around if anyone gets tired."

None of them answered, just carried on bailing, getting slower and lifting less water each time. There were plenty of other boats around, in the distance, but Conner didn't want to be rescued, he wanted to get himself out of danger. Besides, they had no method of contacting anyone for help, except their voices. A mistake he took on his own shoulders.

"If we have to swim, stay together," Jenna advised, "let your lifejacket support you, then use your legs to move and your arms to grab onto something, or someone. If you feel the current pulling you away from where you're headed, swim diagonally across it, don't fight it directly because you won't win."

"But let's not do that except as a last resort, we don't want to lose the 'eggy Su'." Conner said with some emotion.

His words seemed to encourage the others, and the bailing grew faster, at least for a while. As they neared the leeward side of the island, the waves began to calm and the danger of being swamped lessened. The water was still pouring in, and those bailing were now gasping for breath. The harbor wall came into view, and at that exact moment the motor cut out with a crack of electricity and the acrid smell of melted electronics.

As agreed, Conner and Ryan grabbed up the oars, fitted them in the oarlocks and began to propel them towards safety. Each stroke, each scoopful of water burned their arms, it felt like they were climbing a steep cliff. As the harbor drew closer, only Ryan was able to carry on with any speed, his new teenage muscles being tested for the first time.

"Come on, Con." Ryan glanced over at his friend. "I told you I was stronger than you, we're going in circles." He tried to laugh, but it came out as more of a wheeze.

Conner dug deeper and managed to produce a final flurry of strokes that brought them into the sanctuary of the harbor. His arms felt like they were twice as heavy and were going numb. Dawn steered them towards the slipway instead of their usual spot. The 'eggy Su's thwarts were barely above water when the hull ground against it and finally stopped sinking. The teens were lathered in sweat, hot and thirsty, and greatly relieved. They took some time to get their breath back, then wordlessly climbed out one by one. Dawn grabbed the bow rope and tied it off on a mooring ring. They found some dry ground and collapsed onto it. Once they had enough energy, each of them did the same thing; checked their phones.

Although much if their stuff was wet, they'd been able to keep their technology out of the water. Dawn's notebooks had suffered, and their lunch was ruined, but they were safe. Dawn found a pencil and small patch of dry paper, and wrote 'waterproof phone case', underlining it three times.

They were young and so recovered quickly, physically and mentally. After telling the prof what had happened, they all returned to the 'eggy Su' to see what had gone wrong with the boat, all suspecting the same thing; sabotage. They winched the leaky boat out of the sea slowly, allowing as much water as they could to drain out. Jenna retrieved her t-shirt, holding up the sodden garment with a sad look on her face.

"Don't worry," Dawn said, "I'm sure it just needs a good wash. It's only sea water."

Jenna sighed, "It's ruined. Tiny particles of dirt get into the weave and you can't get them out, no matter how much you wash it. I won't be able to wear it again, it will make me itch. I'll just give it to the charity shop."

Dawn laughed and gave Jenna a quick hug. "We'll all chip in, buy you a new one."

This put the smile back on Jenna's face, and they all turned back to the business in hand. Once the boat was clear of the water, they emptied it out and, using the winch, rolled it onto its side. There was a split almost a yard long in the center of the hull, running bow to stern. Each end of it was an irregular tear, but the middle section was cut straight and true. Terry looked closer, then pointed. "See here, these scratches are all regular and parallel. That was done with a saw blade."

"Sabotage then, must have been done last night." Conner sounded angry.

Dawn looked at the hull, a puzzled look on her face, "so why didn't it sink in the harbor?"

"Maybe she, assuming it was Verbena, put some tape over it, something that would fall off once we were moving," Terry guessed.

Ryan removed the batteries and left them in the shade to dry, then dismantled the control electronics. The housing had been designed to be water-resistant, not actually watertight and a lot of the sea spray had got inside. "The good news is, it's fixable. The bad news is I can't do it here, so it looks like we're rowing back."

"Don't be silly, I'll give you a tow," the prof said, smiling broadly. "And I'm putting you in charge of the island's new electronics repair shop." He patted Ryan on the back.

Ryan's smile slowly faded. "There's no room, do we have to build the shop first?"

The BoatProf laughed loudly. "No, I'm expecting a delivery in the next few days, something completely suitable for what we need."

The prof grew serious. "By the way, we had a visitor last night. The dogs went wild just after midnight, I let them out and they went racing down to the beach. By the time I'd got myself down there, whoever it was had gone. The dogs were sniffing around and they mostly obliterated any footprints. I did find a single print near the waterline. It was a bit scuffed, but it looked like a hiking boot or something substantial like that."

"Could it have been military style?" Terry asked.

"Yes, yes it could have been I suppose. Someone you know?" The prof asked, a slight smile on his face.

"Possibly, we don't know for sure."

"Well, you be careful, all of you." The prof looked them all in the eye one by one until he'd got some form of agreement from each. "Now, let's go and fix that hull of yours, I have just the right stuff and a trick I learned several years ago."

The 'stuff' turned out to be epoxy resin made to the prof's own recipe and strips of what looked like thin bandages. It smelled so bad they had to work on it outside and while wearing dust masks. Working from both sides, the split was soon sealed and was stronger than the rest of the boat, according to the professor. As it was a chemical reaction, the 'eggy Su' was sea-worthy again in only a few hours.

Once this was done, they returned to their interrupted conversation and spent the rest of the day planning out what they would need for the upcoming spy mission, but agreed to ask around to see if anyone would loan them a camera with a telephoto lens. It would be much easier that way, and with considerably less risk. As usual, they'd tell their parents they would be camping out on Moon Crescent Beach, which would actually be true, at least after their adventure.

At one point during the day, Terry disappeared for several minutes, returning with four wooden paddles. He stashed them in the 'eggy Su' then turned to the others to explain. "I borrowed them from the prof. It will be easier and quieter to paddle the boat instead of using those oars. And we'll be able to get closer to the ship."

Conner smiled. "Good thinking. We need every advantage we can get."

At the end of the day, the BoatProf broke out his jet-ski to tow them back home. "It's not as friendly to the environment as your EB, but it does have an impeller and not a propeller, so it's better for sea creatures." He smiled and threw them a line.

The teens climbed into the 'eggy Su' occasionally glancing at the repair to check for leaks. trying not to look down at where the cut had been fixed. There was still a slight chemical smell, but not a drop of water came through it. The 'stuff' proving to be as tough and reliable as the prof had promised.

The BoatProf took a more southerly heading as he towed them back home, taking the jet-ski towards a narrow channel between a series of large rocks that barely jutted out of the sea. The teens were a little worried at how close to the rocks they came, but they trusted the prof to know what he was doing. As they entered the channel fully, both boat and jet-ski were grabbed by the current and dragged along at some speed, certainly better than either engine could manage alone. This wild ride continued for several minutes until they emerged into the open sea on the western side.

"Wow! I've never moved so fast in a boat," Conner grinned.

The prof towed them a few hundred yards further south and pointed to another channel.

"That one takes you north!" he shouted above the engine noise.

Despite the prof's shortcut, it still took them over an hour to get back to the harbor. By the time they reached safety, they were still glancing at the repair from time to time. They all waved and said their thanks and goodbyes as the prof headed off home, leaping the jet-ski over the waves with some speed and skill.

"Ok," conner said seriously, "it's obvious that phones aren't flares, particularly when we don't have a signal. I vote we don't leave the harbor again until we have some. Agreed?"

"Good idea, buy how much are they?" Ryan asked. "We don't have a lot of money."

"Let's find out," Dawn said. "Our lives are worth more than a few dollars."

"I agree," Jenna nodded. "Let's learn from our near miss."

"And let's add 'check the hull' to Conner's pre-launch list." Terry said.

They all headed home and spent the night researching flares. Dozens of messages passed between them until they agreed which ones they'd get. For the price of a small pizza each, they were able to buy a water-tight container of mixed flares suitable for their circumstances.

CHAPTER EIGHT
TAKING COUNCIL

GO OVERBOARD

To go overboard simply refers to someone or something accidentally falling off a ship.

While this meaning remains in use, the phrase now has a second and very different meaning. Someone is said to have gone overboard if they've over-spent, been extravagant or done something a long way beyond what is considered normal.

As it turned out, none of them knew anyone who had a proper camera and a long telephoto lens except Terry. His uncle was a keen amateur photographer, but he was unwilling to lend such expensive equipment to the teens for something they were reluctant to talk about. So, they had to do it Terry's way, and take the 'eggy Su' out after the yacht when it left the marina. Weather permitting.

Despite the exclusive nature of the party, it seemed those who were attending wanted to brag about it all over social media. The teens soon discovered it started at six o'clock with cocktails on the main deck, a buffet dinner at seven, and then the moonlight cruise starting at eight. At ten o'clock there would be a 'spectacular' surprise event to finish off the night, followed by a return to the marina.

On Saturday morning, the teens took the 'eggy Su' down to the marina to check out the yacht. As it turned out, it wasn't a super yacht or even anything special, just a fairly new ship of the largest size the marina could handle. It wasn't actually a yacht, it didn't have sails, but looked like a small cruise ship. The 'eggy Su' was still tiny in comparison. The private vessel was cordoned off already, with several vans queued up to deliver food, alcohol and flowers. A private security guard stood there with a clipboard, and they could see several people moving around on the deck and inside the ship. The teens were glad to see they had a very good view of most of the upper deck and inner cabins, even from so low down in the water. In this situation, the need for the rich to show off their wealth would work to their advantage.

The sea was very calm today, something the teens were thankful for. The larger ship could handle a rough sea much better than they could, and big waves throwing the 'eggy Su' around would have made getting sharp images more difficult. They took the boat back to the harbor, and Ryan removed the rechargeable batteries to take home and make sure they were full. Although they had no idea where the yacht would go, they suspected it would stay in the calmer waters close to shore. Most of the guests, they supposed, weren't used to sea travel and so seasickness had to be minimised. They had to be ready for anything though, so Ryan squeezed as much power into the batteries as they would take.

Later that day, the teens returned to the marina. The vans had all gone but the security guard remained. The ship was now smothered in flowers, ribbons and decorative flags. The gang plank was similarly dressed and someone could be seen in the shadowed doorway within the yacht, no doubt waiting to greet the guests and check their invites. They observed all this as they drifted by, just one of many other boats trying to get a good look at this swanky new yacht, and possibly spot someone famous. The group soon got tired of the game and found a shady spot under a jetty a suitable distance away, and settled down to wait.

The guests started arriving at exactly six o'clock. Although most of the guests lived in Stonehaven, and some of them actually within sight of the marina, they all arrived in cars, some complete with chauffeurs. None of them were identifiable from this distance, even by Terry, but he did see something.

"Look, there on the end of the gang plank, do you see someone with red hair?"

They all looked, Dawn taking out her phone and zooming in. "Yes, a tall woman, with red hair, can't really see much more detail." She took a few photos anyway.

Conner nodded, "that's a good start. We just need to confirm it's Renzo's cousin Verbena."

They waited impatiently until 8 o'clock, when the ship's engines roared into life and shortly after the large vessel cast off. They let it get out of the marina and onto the open sea before following as there was no danger of losing it. The yacht was garishly decked out and lit up like a Christmas tree, booming loud music, travelling at only a few knots and leaving a wide wake of churned up water.

Terry had told them to dress in dark clothing and put their phones on silent. "And try not to speak unless you have to, the human voice is one of the most recognisable things to humans, obviously."

The 'eggy Su' slipped out of its hiding place, virtually silent and leaving barely a trace of its passing. Conner slowly guided it towards the port side of the larger vessel, keeping out of the wake. The teens were as silent as the boat, ready with their phones. They caught up with the ship and began edging closer. Conner concentrated on steering the boat, Terry was on lookout, and the rest would take as much video as possible, starting with everyone they could see on the deck.

As it was still daylight, the teens would be fully visible to anyone who looked in their direction. Although the guests weren't paying attention, the ship still had a captain and crew. Most of their eyes would be focused on the front of the ship and where it was going, as well as on their instruments. The teens were pretty sure the ship's radar wouldn't be able to spot them, being so close to the vessel and so small. They'd soon find out if they were wrong.

Conner aimed astern and brought the 'eggy Su' right up to the yacht's hull, being carefully not to run into it. Luckily for them, the ship's engines made more than enough noise to drown out any sounds they made. Conner feathered the throttle and brought the boat to a point under one of the portholes with a light showing inside. Jenna lifted her phone on the selfie stick and took a few shots. She then lowered the phone and checked what she'd got. She gave the thumbs down signal and Conner moved them on to the next one. The same thing happened twice more, then Jenna found a small office with people coming and going. She took a few minutes of video, and then Conner moved them again.

There was a sound directly above them and they all froze. Like most ships, this one had straight sides with no overhang. If someone bothered to lean over the rail and look down, they'd be spotted. Terry was right, the sound of human voices was clear even above all the other noises.

Someone shouted, "Verbena!" There was a drone of conversation they couldn't quite make out, a male voice, then Verbena answering. The man interrupted her, his voice raised, "you've barely done anything, why do you need a break?"

"Because it's boring, your so-called friends are so dull! I don't call checking invitations and fetching drinks a job."

"You should be grateful I gave you the job with your record. There are plenty of other people looking for work out there and they don't have your anger issues! Now get back to what you're supposed to be doing."

Verbena snapped out "ok!" and then a door slammed shut.

There was a slight pause and then Verbena added "yes, boss, whatever you say, boss. I'll show you grateful."

No one replied; Conner got the impression the last part was sarcasm aimed at someone who was no longer there. After another pause, the door was slammed again, harder this time, and whoever had been there was gone. The teens all exchanged glances, but they would have to discuss that conversation later.

Conner moved the boat to the next porthole and held it steady. Jenna repeated her actions, then smiled widely as she checked what she'd captured. She gave the thumbs up sign and raised her phone again, signalling for Conner to hold position. She couldn't quite see exactly what she was videoing as the phone was at the wrong angle, but she could see enough to frame the shot and not record the side of the ship. When she thought she had enough, she lowered the phone and watched the video. Her eyes widened, then she turned it for the others to see. The Kneasleys were sitting together at one end of the cabin, chatting with two other people on the couch opposite. The man and woman seemed very relaxed, leaning back, drinks in their hands and smiling broadly. Dawn recognized them both straight away from their publicity shots; they were council members. Near the end of the video, just for a few brief seconds, the red-haired woman appeared and said something to the Kneasleys. They saw her face as clear as day, and she didn't look happy, particularly when Renzo dismissed her with an impatient wave.

Jenna immediately copied the footage to Dawn's phone via Bluetooth so they had a backup. Conner moved the boat over to the next lit porthole, although he doubted whether they'd find anything as juicy as in the previous one. The next cabin was a staff lounge. Jenna took some video anyway, and they moved on again.

At this point the ship began to turn a wide arc towards the east. It was barely 9 o'clock, so they doubted the ship was returning to the marina. Conner dropped back at this point, they wanted to look in the portholes on the starboard side, which meant crossing the wake. It was better to allow the sea to settle a little before taking their small boat over the churned-up waves.

Several minutes later the 'eggy Su' was lifted and pushed around a little, but nothing the teens weren't used to. Conner increased speed slightly and once again caught up with the yacht as stealthily as he could manage. This time, Dawn was on the side facing the hull, so she lifted her own selfie stick and began to take video of the portholes on this side. They got some good clear shots of the people within, but didn't recognize any of them. The ship carried on east, then began to turn towards the south. Conner followed it around, but they felt they had as much as they were going to get. The Sun was low in the sky now, touching the horizon. The light and heat of the day began to fade as dusk arrived.

Although their task was complete, the teens stayed with the ship as it continued its journey. Each was silent and lost in their own thoughts as they waited for the sun to set and the 'spectacular' surprise. The music fell silent and the engines stopped at almost the same time, at exactly 10 o'clock. Conner immediately cut the throttle, but the motor carried on humming until he flicked the power switch. The ship continued to move forward under its own momentum, gradually leaving the smaller boat behind. Terry indicated the paddles, picking one up himself and quietly lowering it into the water. Dawn, Ryan and Jenna copied him, while Conner worked the tiller. After a few strokes they managed to work up enough speed to maintain their position alongside the yacht.

The ship gradually slowed almost to a stop, moved only by the current. The anchors dropped into the sea with a huge splash and a rattling of chains that made the teens jump. Luckily, they weren't anywhere near them at the time. A few minutes went by and then a massive explosion lit up the sky. The teens jumped again, almost causing them to drop the paddles. Another boom followed, then another, each sending showers of color across the starry sky and outlining the ship in reds and blues.

Conner grinned and whispered, "fireworks. Where are they coming from?"

Dawn leaned towards him and whispered a reply. "Must be one of the islands, let's go and see."

Conner steered the boat around in a tight arc as the others paddled. He pulled away from the yacht and headed to clear water behind the ship. The pyrotechnic display was very impressive now they could see it properly. Deep booms sounded in sequence, followed seconds later by explosive detonations and blooms of color, like huge flowers that filled the sky. Smaller rockets filled in the layer underneath with crackling white embers, and the island itself was lit up with fans of orange sparks higher than the trees.

Any night vision the teens had was ruined by the bright flashes and bursts of light, but they could easily recognize where the fireworks were coming from. After last year's adventure, there was no mistaking Three Hills Island.

Conner started up the 'eggy Su's' motor and the others stowed the paddles. There was no need for silence or even stealth as they were a good distance away from the yacht and the fireworks were still going.

"I wonder if it was the Kneasleys who bought the island," Jenna said, "or if they just rented it for the night?"

"What was the sale price, sis? A cool million dollars?" Ryan asked, glancing over at his sister.

"Yes, that was the asking price," Dawn replied.

"Weren't your parents handling the sale?" Jenna said, turning to Dawn.

"They were. The owner went with another realtor when it didn't sell. Dad was really angry as they'd put a load of work into it."

The sound of fireworks built to a crescendo and then fell silent. A row of letters was left burning, a flaming 'Goodnight' and what they presumed was supposed to be 'ReKnew'—the Kneasley's recycling business—which hadn't quite worked. The sound of applause and drunken cheering reached them a few moments later. Then the yacht's engines started up, the anchor chains rattled again, and the ship headed slowly back towards the marina. The loud music and flashing lights started up again as the ship moved away from the small boat. The party wasn't yet over for those aboard.

"So," Terry said, "back to camp and look through what we've got over a toasted sandwich?"

"Let's go! I'm starving!" Ryan said.

By the light of the full moon, the group found their way to Moon Crescent Beach and their favorite camping spot. Dawn, with a few hints from Terry, started a small fire with driftwood. Once the tents were up, they all gathered around the fire, drinking from their water bottles and toasting their sandwiches and not really caring what was on them. As they ate they made sure everyone had a copy of all the footage and they looked through it. Cell-phone reception was weak this far out of town, but usable, if you were patient. They were already familiar with Renzo and Regina Kneasley, and with his cousin Verbena Stackpole. They accessed the town council website and began comparing pictures of the officials with what their footage showed.

"Ok, here's one, and another, and another," Dawn said. "Looks like half the council were at the party."

"Yep, I've spotted six, maybe seven so far," Conner said.

"And two of them had a private meeting with the Kneasleys," Dawn pointed out.

"Maybe they all did," Ryan said, "we weren't recording all the time."

"Or maybe they invited all of them so it didn't look suspicious," Dawn said. "There are rules about what they can and can't do while they're in office."

"They probably make up those rules themselves, or at least monitor them," Ryan said cynically. "They'll probably just cover for each other if people start asking question."

"Well, we go with the evidence we have," Jenna said, "and just investigate these two. It will take too long to go chasing after all of them. We can find out if any of the others are involved with whatever is going on here later, if we need to."

"Look," Terry said, turning his phone, "this guy was at the field auction, he bid against Renzo."

"So the auction was phony!" Ryan grinned, "I knew it."

"Looks that way, or at least it wasn't entirely honest," Conner agreed. "Do you know who he is, Terry?"

"No, he's definitely not a councilman, but I can't find him anywhere else," Terry replied. "I'll have to keep looking. He can't just be someone Renzo hired for the day, or he wouldn't have been at the party."

Ryan agreed, "I don't think the Kneasleys have friends, just people who are useful to them."

"Do you think that was Renzo shouting at Verbena?" Dawn asked.

"Sounded like him," Terry replied. "I heard him at the auction. Why do they have to shout all the time, so loud."

"Neither of them was very happy," Jenna said "I wonder what she meant by that 'grateful' comment she made?"

"Sounds like she's up to something," Ryan said with a smile. "I wouldn't trust her."

Conner stretched and yawned widely. "I'm getting tired eyes; I think we should call it done for today and get some sleep. We don't want to miss anything because we can't concentrate."

"Good idea," Jenna agreed, "it seems like there's hours of this stuff. It's going to take a lot of work to go through it all. I wish I could show this to my gran, but she'll want to know how I got it." She stood and walked over to the tent "Dawn, you coming?"

Dawn glanced at Terry, "yes, be there in a sec, just want to check something."

Terry was already wrapped in his emergency blanket. He didn't like tents, he just slept in the open near the fire. His phone was poking out, the screen lighting up his face. Conner and Ryan both went into their own tent, Ryan carrying the last of his food. There was some rustling and mumbled conversations from the two tents as they all got settled, then the teens fell silent. They drifted off to sleep, lulled by the sound of the waves and the soft background noises of the local wildlife.

CHAPTER NINE

ISLAND HOPPING

JURY RIGGING

When a ship loses its main mast, a replacement could be Jury or Jerry Rigged in place to allow the ship to continue its journey.

In modern times, this meaning has spread to other engineering disciplines and is now applied to anything that involves a temporary fix. This could be a physical fix or even something like a software patch.

The teens slept in late on Sunday morning, then assembled around the fire one by one, Ryan last. They divided up the food they had left from the day before, which wasn't much, and toasted it over the small fire. Terry, as usual, had been up for hours. He'd gathered some more wood, rekindled the fire, and was now playing a game on his phone and complaining about his low battery.

"We should put a charge point on the 'eggy Su'" he said to Ryan, "a USB output so we can charge our phones and other stuff."

"Yeah, should be possible, those big batteries can cope with a tiny drain like a phone. I'll see what I can do."

After breakfast, when they were all packed up and the fire put out, they headed back to the 'eggy Su' moored on the beach and loaded up to head back to the harbor. It was about noon when they arrived, so they sat around for a while deciding what to do.

Dawn was sitting with a notebook in one hand and a pencil in the other, which she tapped against her lips as she was thinking. "I've been thinking..." she started.

"I thought I could smell burning," Ryan interrupted with a smirk.

Dawn continued as if he hadn't spoken. "If the Kneasley's have bought Three Hills Island, where did all that money come from, and what are they going to use it for?"

"You think they aren't just going to live there?" Conner said.

"No, that doesn't make any sense. They have that big condo, and all their business is done in town, why would they isolate themselves out there? I don't think they do anything unless they can make money doing it."

"You could be on to something there, Dant," Ryan said.

"Are you thinking we should go and check it out?" Terry asked.

"We should," Dawn nodded.

"I'm just doing a quick search online, see if I can find the island mentioned anywhere." Jenna tapped away at her phone, then began scrolling through the results.

Conner went through his checklist and then switched on the motor. Dawn and Terry untied the mooring ropes and they set off, heading slowly towards the harbor entrance.

"No, there's nothing recent here. They can't have released the news about the sale of the island, or no one cares enough to mention it." Jenna put her phone away in the waterproof case they'd all started using.

With that done, Conner accelerated out onto the open sea. There was barely a swell today, the wind blowing north along the coast and bringing a warm breeze with it. Conner turned them in the rough direction of Three Hills Island, not really needing to check his heading as his familiarity with the Maine coastline increased.

As they drew nearer the island, Terry shaded his eyes against the sun and began to study the area. After a few minutes he spoke. "Something going on around the island. There are a lot of boats there today."

"Can you see who they are?" Conner asked.

"No, keep moving closer, I doubt anyone will notice us."

Conner did as instructed and kept the boat heading straight for the island's small jetty. More details were revealed as they approached. "I see what you mean, who are all those people?"

"There's some big boats there," Terry whispered, "one of them is a cargo barge. There are several water taxis, and some small speed boats. Oh, I see, they're cleaning up the mess from the fireworks display."

"Cool, we can go around the other side and land without being seen," Ryan said.

"Well, let's go around and have a look before we jump to conclusions," Dawn suggested.

"Yes. I'm not sure we should be landing anyway," Jenna added. "Going on private property to rescue someone like we did last year is fine. But I'm not sure we should be doing it without good reason."

"Good point," Conner conceded, "we can have a look though, nothing wrong with that."

Conner turned them away from the island and headed for the open sea to the north, staying a few hundred yards out from the rocky coastline. The work on dismantling the scaffold that had held the fireworks continued; the clang of the metal poles could be heard from a long distance away. There was no other traffic around the rest of the island, just a few tourist boats in the distance and the ever-present container ships on the horizon. They, or rather Terry, did see some people moving about on the island, but he couldn't see what they were doing.

Ryan sighed. "This is a bust, there's nothing suspicious going on here, not now."

"I think you're right," Conner agreed. "I think it was a good idea to check it out though."

"So, what now?" Dawn asked.

"We could go and talk to them," Jenna said.

"Who?"

"The people with the boats."

"What, just go over there and say hi?"

"Sure, but I was thinking more about asking if they have any work for us."

"And then what?" Ryan said.

"And then we do the work and talk to them, see what they're doing and what's going on."

"Do you think they'll tell us, even if they know?" Conner asked.

"There's only one way to find out," Jenna said with a grin.

The others didn't want to go, but couldn't think of a good reason why they shouldn't. People on boats, particularly at sea, were a friendly bunch for the most part. Conner turned the 'eggy Su' to follow the southern side of the island and then around to the small jetty, which was completely hidden by all the boats.

They were ignored until the cargo barge chugged backwards out of the flotilla and slowly turned towards shore. Conner slipped into the gap left behind and someone on the jetty noticed them. A tall man with an old clipboard glanced at them, consulted his list and then looked them over.

"What are you here for?" he said in a neutral tone.

"We were wondering if there were any small jobs you needed doing," Jenna said.

The man smiled. "I see." he looked at his clipboard and then around at the island, then turned back to the teens. "You're a bit too late, most of its done already. We just have to tidy up and we're out of here."

"We can do that," Jenna said quickly.

The man laughed. "Ok. The pyrotechnics crew were here for about three days and they left a mess over there. There's also some boxes and bags blowing around. If you could tidy all that up, that would be great."

"Ok, how much?"

"Hmm, it's only a bit of a job, I'll give you five dollars each."

"Ten."

"Tell you what, I'll give you sixty dollars total and you take all the garbage away with you."

"Done!"

They tied the 'eggy Su' to a mooring ring on the jetty and climbed out with practised ease. The man led them over to a spot near some small trees. The ground was flattened and it looked like an entire class of teens had had a picnic there. "As you can see, this all needs clearing up, it's mostly sandwich containers, so nothing too gross." He pointed to where the last of the scaffold poles were being removed. "When those guys have finished, which shouldn't be much longer, you can grab all the stuff over there. When you're loaded up and ready to go, come see me. Ok?"

"Ok." Jenna smiled.

The man walked away, consulting his clipboard.

Ryan looked at Jenna. "Litter-picking? Really?"

"What? I got us on the island, didn't I?"

"Yeah, but when we volunteer, we do litter-picking all the time."

"But this time we're getting paid to do it," Conner pointed out. "And, we're actually undercover litter-pickers." Conner smiled, but Ryan wasn't convinced.

"Still not happy."

"Let's just get on with it," Dawn said. "Terry can slip away for a scout around while we tidy this up."

Terry smiled. "Good plan." He patted Ryan on the back. "Have fun," he grinned and slipped away between the trees.

"Come on, let's get started," Conner said. "There's not that much here so take it slow."

They each started stacking sandwich containers and coffee cups and squashing them into small take-out bags. Most of the containers were empty, or just had a smear of various sauces in them. As they worked, they tried not to look around, although it was what they were here for. Apart from the clearing-up operation, there didn't seem to be much going on.

With the four of them working it wasn't long before the whole mess was cleared up. They pretended to be looking around for more litter to play for time, although it seemed no one was paying them any attention, not even the man with the clipboard, who was standing on the jetty looking out to sea.

Terry appeared a few moments later, stepping from behind a tree like he'd emerged from the trunk. "There's nothing going on anywhere but here," he said. "I tried to look in the house but the windows are covered over, and there's a boathouse, which is locked up tight."

"It is?" Conner queried. "When I went looking for a phone when we were here with Marty Whitford the side door of the boat-house was open. Did you see the house window with the bars? I looked in there."

"Yes, but the windows look like they've been painted black on the inside."

"That's weird. So, they aren't going to be living here."

"So, what are they doing here?" Dawn asked.

"It looks like nothing to me," Ryan said.

"Maybe that's what it's supposed to look like," Jenna said knowingly.

Conner looked around and noticed the other workers had finished. "Let's go and clean up this last bit, then go and see about getting paid. Looks like there's nothing to see here, not today."

The support scaffold for the fireworks display had been removed now, leaving a wide are of blackened grass and dried mud. Behind this was another flattened area that looked like it had been used to prepare the fireworks. There were small pieces of card, empty duct tape rolls and short lengths of wire everywhere. Some larger boxes had blown into the undergrowth and some bags had become tangled in the trees. The teens picked a large box that was still solid and began filling it with the picnic stuff and the small pieces of junk. Terry and Jenna went over to the trees and started to remove the bags and boxes. It took a little longer to pick up every small piece, but they were soon done. There was nothing they could do about the flattened and scorched grass, but when they'd finished there wasn't a piece of litter anywhere.

With nothing else to do, or pretend to do, they grabbed the garbage and headed back to the jetty. Most of the other boats had left by now, leaving only what they presumed was the tall man's speed boat and a new arrival, a large and brand-new cabin cruiser, gleaming a blue-white in the sun. Several people were climbing out of it onto the jetty, some needing to be helped.

Conner, who was at the front, froze. "It's the Kneasleys!" he hissed.

The others all looked over and saw Renzo and Regina Kneasley walking onto dry land with wide smiles on their faces and heading straight towards them. Behind, and looking less enthusiastic, were the two councillors they'd been seen with on the cruise. Two more people were behind them, looking totally out of place in business suits and ties. The teens turned their faces away, pretending to be doing something with the box.

"They don't know our faces, do they?" Dawn whispered.

"I don't think so, but let's not take any chances," Jenna said.

"It's fine, they aren't even looking this way. Besides, we're only workers, we're beneath their notice," Terry said wisely.

Led by Renzo, the whole party approached the tall man and he and Renzo briefly spoke. Then the party swept on by and headed towards the house without a glance at the teens. The man watched them go, an angry expression on his face. He saw the teens and his frown changed to a smile. "All done?"

"Yes, there's not a scrap of garbage left anywhere," Jenna answered confidently.

"Excellent." He pointed at the box of garbage. "And you're taking that with you?"

"Yes, as agreed."

The man pulled some crumpled notes out of his pocket and counted out sixty dollars in tens. He handed it to Jenna and then pulled a business card from another pocket. This was also crumpled but still legible. "Take this. If you need more work just give me a call; we often need people with boats." The name on the card was Vance Powell, and it said he was an event organizer.

"We will, Vance," Jenna replied.

They all said their goodbyes. Vance climbed into his speedboat and started messing with the outboard. The teens headed towards their boat, loaded up the garbage and then sat down in their usual places.

"Well, we didn't get as much as we were expecting there," Conner said, "but we did get some information."

"And sixty bucks," Ryan grinned.

Conner switched the motor on and moved the 'eggy Su' away from the jetty. He glanced over his shoulder to check there were no other boats, and looked straight into the hostile stare of someone they knew. Conner twisted the throttle all the way and headed out to open sea as fast as he could. The others nearly fell off their seats.

"Woah, Conner, what's the rush?" Ryan said for them all.

"Verbena is right there!"

"Where?"

"On the Kneasley's fancy new boat."

They all looked back towards the jetty. Verbena was still in the same position, a white-knuckle grip on the rail, glaring at them as they powered over the waves away from her at full speed.

"Do you think she'll tell Renzo?" Dawn asked.

"I would think so. She does work for him," Ryan answered.

"Do you think she would have done something if Vance wasn't there?" Jenna asked.

"Maybe. She knows who we are," Conner replied.

"We should be extra careful the next few days," Jenna suggested. "Double check everything, make sure she doesn't try to sabotage us again."

"I just thought of something," Dawn said, her eyes wide. "Verbena is away from her boat, now would be a great time to find it and search it!"

"Yes, it would, but we don't know where it is," Ryan pointed out.

"And it's getting a bit late to go looking," Conner said, "so that will have to wait."

"Talking of looking," Ryan said, "we could buy a pair of binoculars with the sixty dollars."

"Actually, I have my eye on a nice jacket," Jenna said, then quickly added "I'm joking!" when she saw their expressions.

"Good idea, we could look in that chandlery store near the harbor, they have used stuff in there," Conner said.

"They might have an anchor, if there's any money left," Ryan said.

"So, what do we do now?" Dawn asked. "We've confirmed those two councillors are working with the Kneasleys, what's our next step?"

"But we don't know what they're working on," Jenna pointed out, "it might be something perfectly legal."

"Like what?" Conners asked.

"Well, what if they have come out here to inspect something? Maybe the Kneasleys want to build a hotel on the island, and the councillors have to give their approval."

Dawn nodded in agreement, "that's a very good point."

"We shouldn't have left," Conner said. He looked at Terry. "If we circle back to the island and land on the north side, do you think you can get close enough to hear what they're saying?"

Terry shrugged. "It depends on how close I can get, how loud they're talking, and if they're moving around. I'll give it a go."

"It might look suspicious if they catch him on his own," Jenna said.

"We could all go, just say we're on litter patrol, which could be true," Ryan grinned.

"Yes, stay together as long as we can, and Terry can go solo for the close-up work," Conner nodded, turning the 'eggy Su' back towards the north shore in a wide arc.

"Let's hope we can back in time," Dawn said.

"Shouldn't take too long," Conner said. "And now we have another reason to be glad we went electric. We can slip back to the island unnoticed."

Ryan smiled. "It's nice to be appreciated."

It took them a while to get back to the island as Conner kept them a good way out. Once the jetty was out of sight, he was able to head more directly ashore. They soon passed the place where, the previous summer, they'd found Marty Whitford's damaged rigid inflatable boat. There was a narrow channel between two of the three hills that made up the island. The RIB had been torn open on the sharp rocks, so they knew not to try landing there.

Instead, Conner steered them around to the eastern side and landed them on a smooth, sloping rock just large enough for them to moor up and climb out. With the 'eggy Su' secured bow and stern, the teens moved off into the undergrowth that came almost down to the sea here. Terry took the lead, moving a few paces ahead. When they came to an open area, Terry signalled for them all to wait while he scanned the area. He could see the house up ahead, but no sign of movement. They all moved rapidly across the open section and took cover in some tall bushes. Repeating this a few more times, they finally saw movement. The Kneasleys and the two councillors were walking slowly along the path, Renzo gesturing expansively with his arms. The two men in suits were nowhere to be seen.

Terry called them together and whispered, "I think they'll walk straight passed us if we stay here. Be very quiet and still. I'll let you know when it's safe to move. If we spread out along here, we might be able to hear more of their conversation."

"If they do catch us we just say we're working for Vance, picking up litter," Ryan said, which was, or at least had been, true.

"If we need to run, don't go straight back to the boat," Terry advised, "make sure it's clear before going anywhere near it."

They all agreed it was a good plan, and so they took up positions in the undergrowth as far apart as they could manage. Each then settled down in what they considered was a suitable spot. As it was summer, the foliage was thick and the wildlife active, which would help screen them from sight and sound. They all fell silent and waited as the adults moved closer, hoping the small group wouldn't take another path or turn around and head back.

CHAPTER TEN

CHAIN OF CONVERSATION

HITTING A SNAG

*The original meaning of the word snag was a sharp object,
generally a tree trunk or similar, that affected
the ships ability to carry on.*

*This definition has expanded in modern times to include
anything that stops a task being completed, whether
it's a physical object or something less defined.*

Terry had chosen to stand upright behind a native oak tree, its trunk screened from the path by a decorative bush. He slowly took a deep breath, then let it out, relaxing his shoulders as he did so. Around him he could hear the others settling down, a bird hunting insects on the ground a few yards away, and the slow droning of a bee above his head. There was a strong smell coming from the flowers, brought to him by the soft breeze blowing across his face. Under his hands, he could feel the rough bark of the tree, and the slight tickle of a tiny insect against his skin. With that done, he concentrated only on his hearing, his other senses alert but secondary. He heard footsteps approaching, four pairs of shoes thumping on the dry mud trail worn through the short grass. They were moving quite fast, so this was no relaxed walk around the island. The hum of human voices grew louder, the words not yet discernible. As the seconds slipped by, the sounds became words, although not yet a full conversation. A man was speaking, the same voice they'd heard when following the ship.

There was a hint of movement and shadows danced across the foliage to Terry's right. He caught the first glimpse of the four adults. Renzo and Regina Kneasley were walking together, as were the two councillors, a distinct gap between them. Renzo was talking, gesturing with his hands. "… already a done deal. Everything is in place for a trial run and then off we go."

Someone mumbled, a woman's voice.

Renzo replied, "I'd like to think so, but who can tell." There was silence for a few moments, then Renzo spoke again. "The rest is up to you; everything is done at my end."

One of the councillors spoke, a woman with curly brown hair and a very serious expression on her face. "As I said, the initial documents have gone through, but we're still waiting on the next payment."

They were passing directly in front of him now, only a couple of yards between him and the nearest adult. The breeze carried a strong scent of someone's musky aftershave, so strong it over-powered the smells of nature. The shadows moved on, the stilted conversation continuing.

Conner was squatting behind a low bush, peering through the gaps in the leaves and wishing he'd chosen to stand. His knees were starting to hurt, but he couldn't move as the Kneasleys were right there. He couldn't see Terry, somewhere off to his right, but that wasn't surprising. Ryan was to his left, and, as usual, didn't seem to be taking the whole thing seriously. Trying to concentrate on his own task and not worry about anyone else, Conner listened as hard as he could, wishing he'd thought about taking out his phone and recording the conversation. Then again, he'd probably get an alert and his phone would beep.

"… but we're still waiting on the next payment."

"I told you it will be with you as soon as I'm satisfied and not before."

"And when will that be? We're taking a big risk here."

Ryan was sitting on the ground, his back to a tree. He was really hungry now, and was just hoping his stomach wasn't going to rumble. He was thinking about how, if they'd planned better, they could have brought a microphone with a parabolic reflector and listened to the whole conversation from hundreds of yards away. They could probably even have stayed on the 'eggy Su' and recorded the whole thing while sitting safely out to sea. They really did need to get more gadgets if they were going to do this sort of thing every summer. Moving shadows passed quickly over his hiding place, and Ryan was reminded of what they were doing.

"… taking a big risk here."

"Like I said, when I'm satisfied, but hopefully within the next few days."

"You said that yesterday. We don't want to call this deal off, but we will if we think you're playing us for fools."

Dawn was kneeling on two pages torn from an old notebook behind a thick bush with glossy leaves. She'd seen them the last time she was here, and had wondered what they were. She'd discovered they were called Rhododendrons, which apparently meant 'rose tree'. They were originally from Asia, but could now be found all over the world. They were popular with gardeners because they were easy to grow and had masses of brightly coloured flowers in spring and summer. This one had white flowers on it, mostly fading as the season wore on. As the Kneasley party approached, Dawn listened carefully and began taking notes as best she could in the low light.

"… playing us for fools."

"Linda, please, don't be like that. We all stand to benefit from this, and it won't work unless we're all in."

"I know that, but me and Max here are the ones taking the biggest risk. Our reputations are on the line."

"Exactly!" Max agreed with a nod. He was a short man with a mop of black hair which swayed when he moved his head.

Jenna was standing crouched over behind a clump of saplings and wishing she was somewhere else. The ground was muddy, the trees were dirty and there were insects everywhere. She didn't mind getting dirt on her skin, because it came off, skin and all. But dirty clothes were never completely clean again. She tried not to think about it, instead holding out her phone and recording the nearby conversation as best she could. A spider crawled up the trunk of the nearest tree. In her mind it was huge and hairy and had far too many beady eyes. She shuffled away from it, and stood on a dry twig. The crack sounded very loud to Jenna. She froze, one hand over her mouth.

"Exactly!" There was a short pause and then Max added "and your other problem?"

"That's not a problem, just a temporary glitch." Renzo stopped and looked towards the bushes, "what was that?"

The others stopped and copied Renzo as he peered into the undergrowth, his head lowered and his neck craning forwards. The silence stretched, broken only by the buzzing of insects and the slight rustle of the breeze through the foliage. Renzo took a few steps closer, moving his head from side to side to look around the trunks. It was gloomy in the undergrowth, and his eyes were adapted to the brightness of the sunny day. All he could see were dark shadows.

Linda turned back to Renzo with an impatient sigh. "It's nothing. Stop trying to distract us. Is Verbena going to be a problem, yes or no?"

Renzo looked angry as he turned to face her. "She's family, I'll take care of it and you don't need to worry about her."

Linda held up her hands in submission. "Ok, if you say so. I won't mention it again."

"Good, I'd appreciate it," Renzo snapped.

There was an awkward silence, which continued as the four adults moved away, the Kneasleys leading, the councillors lagging behind, holding a whispered conversation. It only took them a few minutes to walk along the trail and disappear around the other side of the island. Terry called the all clear and they gathered behind a thick bush, rubbing their knees and stretching.

"I'm so sorry," Jenna said. "There was a huge spider. I only moved my foot a few inches…"

"Let's get back to the 'eggy Su' and get out of here. We can talk about it when we're safely out at sea." Terry whispered, leading them through the undergrowth and back towards the boat.

"But it was huge," Jenna hissed at their retreating backs, then ran to catch up. "As big as my thumb, with loads of eyes and it was looking at me!"

Terry returned to the shoreline just above the 'eggy Su's mooring place. Keeping himself concealed behind a tree, he surveyed the area, seeing and hearing nothing out of place. With a gesture to the others, he slowly moved down the shore and began untying the bow line. The others followed, climbing into the boat; Jenna detaching the stern line and then jumping into her seat. With sighs of relief, Conner moved them away from the shore and headed back towards the harbor and home.

"So Jenna, tell us about this monster spider." Ryan grinned.

Jenna half-turned in her seat so she could see them all. "It was huge, as big as my phone, sort of black and brown and had hundreds of eyes and it was looking at me in a really aggressive manner."

The others laughed.

"Sounds like a bird-eating tarantula," Terry said, "native to the northern areas of South America."

"Well, it could easily have got here on a ship, or maybe it was someone's pet that escaped." Jenna said.

"Or maybe the Kneasleys are smuggling them in to secretly release in the town and then charge people to remove them, like pest control do with roaches." Ryan laughed.

"That could be their plan, to breed giant spiders and take over the world!" Dawn giggled.

"Ok. Back to more important business," Conner said. "Let's compare notes on what we heard, see if we can make sense of this WEB of crime."

The others groaned, and Jenna mumbled "it wasn't funny," but was smiling when she said it.

Once they were in open water and Conner didn't have to pay full attention to where they were going, they reconstructed the whole conversation from their memories and notes and Jenna's recording.

"We did miss most of what they'd been talking about," Dawn said, "but there's some juicy information here. 'Linda' is Linda DeLong, you can see her picture on the Stonehaven website and she's in the picture we took with the Kneasleys on the cruise ship."

"Cool, we were right!" Ryan smiled.

"Yep. And Max is Maxim Dez... hn... yov–Dezhnyov I think. Anyway, it's him in the picture as well."

"Two for two," Ryan said.

"Yep," Dawn nodded. "But what about this last part, about Verbena. I wonder what she's done?"

"She's probably just been complaining, like she was on the ship," Ryan said.

"What if it's more than that?" Conner said. "What if she's been demanding more money or something?"

"Sounds about right, from what we know of her," Ryan agreed.

"So, we're really not much further forwards," Jenna pointed out. "And this conversation won't stand up as evidence. What we need is proper, solid proof to show the police."

"If Verbena is up to something," Conner said, thinking out loud, "she wouldn't go to the police, because she'd get herself in trouble."

"Are you thinking blackmail?" Ryan said.

"Yes. That would fit what we know." Conner nodded.

"Which means," Dawn said as they were all thinking it, "she must have something to blackmail them with, which will probably be on her boat."

"So, she's not just hiding from the police, she's keeping secrets from the Kneasleys," Terry said. "We really need to find that boat before anyone else does, or find Verbena and follow her until we do find it."

Conner pulled out his phone and found a map of the area. "We know she is, or was, along here somewhere, it's just a matter of where. What we need is a proper chart, not these online maps. Like an older version."

"A visit to Rogue Island then?" Ryan suggested.

"That's what I was thinking, maybe the prof has some and can help us with them."

"It's worth a try."

"Ok, first thing tomorrow, we head off the see the BoatProf and then plan from there. Agreed?" Conner said.

They all agreed, and, as it was getting late, decided to call it a night and go home. The harbor came into sight, and they were soon within its protective walls. Conner looked back at the 'eggy Su' as they climbed onto the jetty and walked away. The harbor staff were there 24 hours a day, but that hadn't stopped Verbena slashing the hull before. They didn't have anywhere else to put her, so they'd just have to hope Verbena had more serious problems than a few teens snooping around.

As they walked through the familiar streets of Stonehaven, they chatted about what they'd heard.

"Did you notice," Dawn said, "that while we were listening, Regina didn't speak."

"Yes," Jenna replied, "you're right."

"That's how they do it," Ryan said.

Dawn looked over at her brother. "Do what?"

"When a couple do that kind of stuff, one of them is clean and one is dirty. That way, Renzo, in this case, can take the fall and say Regina didn't know anything about it. So only one of them goes to jail and they're able to hide some of their loot. Remember last year when we found that barn full of bubble-wrap? That was in Regina's name to keep it separate from Renzo's business."

"How do you know all this?" Dawn asked.

"Because I watch stuff online, crime documentaries and stuff," Ryan explained. "You know, most criminals are dumb and get caught by doing stupid things. People like the Kneasleys are smarter and get away with all kinds of stuff. They get caught by flashing their money around, showing off their success until the police get suspicious."

"Showing off like having huge fireworks displays and moonlight cruises?" Conner said.

"Exactly."

Early the next morning, the teens took the 'eggy Su' and headed off to Rogue Island. Their familiarity with the route and the secret tidal channels the prof had shown them had cut their journey time to less than an hour. Recently, they'd begun to swap positions in the boat so each of them had a go on the tiller or acting as lookout. Ryan also explained to them how he'd wired up the electronics, and what some of the faults were that could be solved on the go. Terry also continued with his Abenaki-Penobscot lessons as he himself improved. Jenna had taken it on herself to teach them to swim better and generally get more exercise, which they did on and near the beach on Rogue Island. Dawn had become the self-appointed keeper of knowledge, and often borrowed Conner's maritime book and tested them all on its contents.

Once they'd reached the island and plugged the 'eggy Su' into the charging point, they went in search of the professor. As it turned out, he was waiting for them to show up, as he had a surprise for them.

"Hello all. Good to see you. I have something to show you, it arrived yesterday," the prof smiled and tapped his nose with his index finger, "a favor for a favor, so to speak."

The teens followed him as he walked past all the assorted buildings that made up the academy, and there on the end was a new structure. "I promised you an electronics workshop, and here it is!" He gestured proudly towards what looked like an airplane had crashed into a pile of railway sleepers. The wings and tail were missing, leaving a mostly intact fuselage, painted a deep blue with a lighter blue stripe down the middle. It was covered in scratches and small dents after a long life of flying.

"Now, I know what you're thinking, 'it's a plane, not a boat.' Actually, it's a sea plane, or at least the front half of one. You can tell by the hull under the cockpit, see? These things are very difficult to recycle because of the materials used, so they slice them up and sell them for use as offices and such. It needs fitting out, but I'm sure you'll all have fun doing that." He smiled widely and looked at each of them.

The teens smiled uncertainly, but had to admit it was a cool thing to have. Ryan was the first to go inside, entering through the hole left when the tail section had been cut off. The plane was a shell inside, not so much as a single piece of wire remained. "This could work," he nodded. "There's plenty of room, it's watertight and solid, we can mount workbenches and stuff along the walls. Probably need to make a wall and a door back there."

"I'm glad you like it," the prof said. "You can help yourselves to wood from the store, there's plenty of pine in there, which is good enough to fill in a hole. I'll get you started and then leave you to it."

Before the professor could leave, they told him their problem with the maps and asked if he had any more accurate charts. He didn't ask any questions, just smiled broadly and led them over to the classroom, relishing the opportunity to show off his charts and to make the most of teaching his students how to read them.

The charts, old and new, were kept on a rack, rolled up in leather tubes. They were well-looked after and not at all damaged or brittle as the teens expected. The rack was immaculately labeled and cross-indexed, which pleased Jenna, and they soon had the right one. Spreading it on a chart table, they all gathered around and found the piece of coast they were looking for. They noticed immediately that instead of the large area of blue that signified the sea on most maps, the chart had numbers, lines, symbols and markings all over it. The prof told them what they all meant and how to interpret them.

It soon became clear that the stretch of coastline they were interested in, between the beach and the marina, wasn't just a straight line after all, but a series of small inlets, now overgrown and hidden by trees and bushes.

"Well, no wonder she disappeared," Ryan said, "you could hide a ship in there."

"Not quite, they're all fairly small, and the water is very shallow there." Dawn pointed out. "But I can understand why she chose to hide there."

"I wonder how she knew about it," Terry said. "We've lived here all our lives and we didn't know it was like that."

"True," Dawn said. "She might have lived in that area as a kid or something."

"However she knows, it looks like we'll have to go in there and find her," Conner said.

"And then wait for her to leave so we can search her boat," Terry added. "She'll have to go out to get food and other supplies at some point, even if it's at two in the morning."

"And hopefully we'll find all the evidence we need to convict every one of them," Jenna said with some feeling.

CHAPTER ELEVEN

LOOKING FOR TROUBLE

RUMMAGE AROUND

*A ships crew might rummage or rummage around
in the hold. This meant moving the cargo from one
place to another, either for balance, to make more space,
or to move the cargo out of a wet spot. A rummage sale
was the selling off of cargo confiscated by the authorities
or simply unclaimed.*

*The modern meaning has expanded to mean moving
a disorderly pile of items around without purpose
or with the hope of finding something useful by chance.*

The teens were all sitting in the 'eggy Su' planning what they needed for their hunt when a familiar figure approached along the jetty and sat on one of the uprights.

"There you are," Aksel said, "I've been looking for you for a few days."

"Oh, we've been a bit busy," Conner replied.

"With a boat we're building," Dawn added hastily.

"Ok, interesting. So you haven't seen anything suspicious around the harbor?"

"Around the harbor, no, nothing." Conner said.

Aksel was carrying a lump of metal, painted black and looking very heavy. He put it down on the jetty. "Someone attached this to our hull. It's a rare earth magnet, a very strong one. We don't know how long it's been there, but we've been getting strange readings for days. We've wasted over a week trying to track down faults in our equipment and it was this all along."

"More sabotage then," Conner stated.

"Yes, it's really getting annoying." Aksel looked at Conner and lowered his voice. "I don't suppose you would know anything, dug up some information that might lead to the saboteurs?"

They all exchanged glances, then Conner spoke for them all. "We're only kids, we don't know anything. If I had to guess, though, I would say the saboteurs will be caught soon."

Aksel nodded, "Ok, that's something at least. So, how would you like to earn some money?"

Ryan spoke up quickly. "Yes."

Aksel laughed. "Well, that was easy." He pulled a small object out of his pocket. It was a dark red sphere, a little smaller than a tennis ball and with a number burned into it. "This is an aquasphere, or sea ball if you prefer. We've been using these to trace the movement of the tides and currents. We throw them in the sea and then wait until they turn up again. Unfortunately, someone has been finding them and moving them around, spoiling our data sets. If you could go looking for them and find them before anyone else, it will increase our accuracy. Most of them will be along the beaches, but you might find some around the islands. And, of course, we lose a lot of them. Even finding one will help. I'll give you a dollar for each one you log."

"Isn't that just adding to the pollution?" Terry asked.

"Oh, no, they're made of wood, either driftwood or local timber. We die them with beet juice and the number is pyrographed into them." Aksel smiled, "it's all 100% natural and biodegradable."

"Ok, we're in," Conner said.

"Great, just remember to take a note of your GPS coordinates and the number on the ball."

Dawn smiled, "I'll make sure we do."

Aksel stood to leave, "do you want this magnet? I'm certainly not taking it back to the ship."

"Sure," Ryan said, "could be useful."

"Good luck." Aksel saluted and walked away.

Ryan stood and retrieved the magnet. "Wow, that's heavy, maybe it will work as an anchor."

"It certainly will if we anchor to something metal," Terry said.

"As long as we can get it off again."

"You know," Conner said, glancing up from his maritime book, "all this anchoring business isn't as easy as you think."

The others all looked at him as he paused to see if he had their attention.

"It's not?" Ryan asked with a slight hint of curiosity.

"No. For one thing, the rode is as important as the anchor. It has to be the right length, which is as much as ten times the depth of the water."

"Ten times?" Ryan was surprised. "So even in ten feet of water we'd need one hundred feet of rode?"

"Yes, more in rough weather. The long rode lets the anchor sit correctly on the sea bed, which makes it harder to move. And the type of anchor you have also matters. Different ones like claw, plow, and mushroom are used for different things like sand, mud and rock. The whole thing together, anchor and rode, is called 'ground tackle'."

"Sounds like a sports term," Jenna smiled.

"Always anchor into the wind, and tie the rode to the bow, not the stern. Leave enough room for the vessel to turn a full 360 degree circle on the tide or winds." Conner looked at Ryan, "And lower the anchor into the water, don't just throw it."

"Why are you looking at me?"

"And," Conner emphasised, "make sure the rode isn't wrapped around something that can be pulled overboard, like your legs."

"That makes sense," Dawn agreed.

"The curve on the rode is known mathematically as a 'catenary curve', from 'catena', the Latin word for chain... wow, that's a serious equation, I don't think we need to learn that bit." Conner turned the book around to show the others.

Only Dawn studied it for more than a few seconds. "Hmm, interesting."

The teens' short maritime lesson was interrupted by more visitors. Matias and Teuila arrived looking very serious. The boys, who had been slouching, immediately sat upright and smiled. The couple approached and stood above them on the jetty.

"Hi everyone. We came around yesterday, but you weren't here," Matias said quietly.

"We've been a bit busy, with our new boat," Conner said.

Dawn, who picked up on their mood, said, "what's wrong?"

Teuila answered. "We've had a break-in, while we were out. Someone came into the workshop and wiped all our data."

"Oh no!" Dawn gasped.

"Luckily, we had most of it backed up to the cloud," Matias said, "but it's scary to think someone just walked in, knowing what we were doing and when we were out."

"We've changed the locks, strengthened everything," Teuila said.

"And now I find myself making a backup every few minutes, just in case." Matias pulled a USB data drive out of his pocket. "I take this everywhere."

"Yeah, Aksel had a problem as well," Ryan lifted up the magnet. "Someone attached this to their hull, messed up their equipment."

"I've had enough of this. Did you see anything at all?" Matias asked.

Conner gave their stock answer, his voice a monotone. "We're only kids, we don't know anything. But if I had to guess, I would bet the saboteurs will soon be caught."

Matias and Teuila shared a look, then smiled slightly. "Yes, we think so too. Be careful, all of you, remember to call for help, should you happen to need any."

They all nodded, while thinking they didn't need any help, they would handle it themselves, like they did last year.

When the couple had gone, Conner turned to the others and quietly said, "I've had enough of this as well. We know we need to find Verbena's boat, or at least Verbena, so we can follow her back to it. Let's get it done today, even if we have to check every inlet and cove in Maine."

The others all agreed, but Ryan said, "what about lunch?"

Dawn reached into her bag and pulled out a small protein bar, which she then threw at Ryan.

"This won't keep me going very long, got any more?"

"No. Don't worry, I'm sure you won't starve between now and dinner time."

"I might," Ryan mumbled.

"Ok," Conner said, "we've got just over half a charge, so we should be fine as we'll be going slowly anyway. Weather's good, lifejackets on, we seem to have gained a sort of anchor to replace Ryan and we have charts in our phones, and... we have flares! Let's go."

Dawn and Terry unfastened the mooring lines with practised ease and Conner headed them out onto the open sea. It was very calm today, and the sun was strong, with barely a breeze to cool them down.

"That's another thing to add to the list: sunblock," Dawn pulled out her note book and wrote it down on a page headed 'new list'.

"That's another reason why we need a solar panel for a roof," Ryan pointed out, "it would give us power, shade in good weather and shelter in bad."

"Well, if we find enough of those sea balls, we can buy one," Jenna was already looking out for them.

It didn't take them long to go past the beach and around the headland. Between it and the marina entrance there was a long stretch of folded coastline filled with places to hide a small boat. They had no choice but to check out every inch until, if their theory was correct, they found their target. It didn't help that the boat was a dirty brown color. The dark rock of the area and the trees and shrubs which grew right to the water's edge would camouflage it nicely.

The sea was relatively busy today, with pleasure craft of all kinds and speeds everywhere they looked. From simple surfboards to small yachts to powerful speedboats, they were all out enjoying themselves. This gave them a small advantage in that they weren't the only boat around, should anyone be looking, but they were the only one so close to the shore. To most visitors to the area, this part of the coast looked hazardous and unnavigable.

The teens' first plan was to casually cruise by close to shore and check the inlets, but they soon realised they couldn't see all the way to land, and, for most of the inlets, they'd have to actually go in to them. They hoped Verbena had merely moored up to a rock or tree, but it was possible there was a small boathouse hidden away somewhere. One or two of the coves they found were obviously unused, as they found out when they got twigs tangled in their hair from the low-hanging branches. In the end, it was this problem that gave them the first clue to Verbena's hideout.

They were heading towards the shore in a narrow inlet about halfway to the marina when Terry hissed, "wait." He pointed to a spot just ahead, "look, those branches all end at the same height, something went through here."

Now that it was pointed out, the others saw it too, a regular line in the overhang, too neat to be natural. Conner steered the boat under the overhang and between the rocky shore and a huge grey boulder like a tiny island. Beyond was a deep cove with a thin strip of sand about ten yards long. The sea was dead calm here, although it still rose and fell with the tide. Moored to a large tree by a long rope was the boat they'd been looking for, which appeared to be even more dirty and rundown now they were closer to it. The only exception was the two outboards, which looked almost brand new.

As soon as Conner's eyes registered the boat was the right one, he slipped the motor into reverse and backed away, out to the open sea. He then moved back to the last cover they'd explored and stopped, partially hidden from view.

Conner leaned forwards and whispered, "What's the plan? Do we go ashore and approach on foot, by sea, or both?"

"Did anyone see if Verbena was there?" Dawn asked, looking mostly at Terry.

He shook his head. "I didn't see her, but there's a lower cabin on that boat, as well as the wheelhouse. The only way we can be sure she isn't there is to go and look through a porthole."

"What if she sees us as we get closer?" Jenna said, "it's not as if we can pretend we're casually passing."

"Ok," Terry said decisively, "I'll go along the shore and see if I can tell if she's in or not. If she is we can watch and hope she goes out, if not one of you can sneak in while I stand watch."

"Ok," Conner said, "I'll turn the boat around so we can make a quick getaway if things go wrong."

With the other four safely ashore, Conner turned the boat around and backed it towards the beach. He moored it up close enough to climb into from the shore, but with the bow pointing to the exit.

Terry led the others through the scrub towards the boat, moving as silent as a shadow. The others followed, trying to emulate his skills and mostly failing. When they got nearer, Terry stopped them with a gesture, and moved ahead a little. He melted into the undergrowth, disappearing from sight.

From where he was hiding, Terry could only see one side of the boat and part of the rear deck. Its bow was pointed out to sea, the mooring line tied with what looked like a quick release knot. A shadow moved across one of the portholes, then the hatch opened very slowly. He could see a mass of red hair, which cautiously rose up and revealed Verbena's face. There was a noise to Terry's right; a disturbance of foliage and some twigs cracking.

A loud roar sent the local wildlife scattering in all directions and caused the teens to dive for cover. Someone shouted up ahead, one of the outboards revved hard and the brown boat shot out of its hiding place and headed out to sea. Two voices shouted after it and two figures appeared, running towards the boat as if they could give chase. They stopped on the edge of the waves, only a few yards from Terry's hiding place. He could smell deodorant and a faint hint of fruity smoke and coffee. They looked around the clearing, giving him a good view of their faces. They looked familiar, but he couldn't remember where he'd seen them before. As if expecting the boat to return, the two men lingered for a while, their shoes sinking in the wet sand. Finally, they left, heading up the hill towards the coastal trail, one blaming the other for giving away their presence. Neither of them sounded particularly sad about the event.

The teens waited several tense minutes, taking their cue from Terry when it was safe to emerge. He gestured for them to stay where they were, then moved forward. After a few more minutes he signalled them over to the space previously occupied by Verbena's camp. It was obvious she'd been here for some time, probably sleeping on the boat but cooking on the small beach. A ring of stones surrounded a fire, which was still smouldering. Discarded take-out containers and other trash surrounded the fire, some of it partially burned. It looked like Verbena had thrown them into the flames and missed and then just left them there. A battered camp stool, partially sunk into the sand, sat next to it. A line had been tied between two trees; several pairs of damp socks hung over it.

The others waited on the edge of the camp as Terry carefully searched it. He laughed as he pointed out some footwear marks. "Shoes, and they were wearing suits, talk about amateur."

"But who were they?" Dawn asked.

"They looked familiar, but I can't remember where I've seen them before."

Ryan turned around, "I'll go get Conner, he's probably wondering what's happening over here."

"There are some nice clear prints here, best take some photos before they dry," Terry said, pulling out his phone.

Ryan returned with Conner. "What happened?" Conner asked, looking around.

"I was moving towards the boat when these two men showed up. They were dressed in suits and shoes. Verbena obviously saw them and ran for it. Maybe she knew them, or maybe she just ran as a precaution."

"She was off like a rocket," Ryan said, "I've never seen anyone move so fast."

"Yeah, that might have been us," Terry said regretfully.

"What do you mean?" Conner said.

"It looked like she was already alert and ready to run. I think she either saw or heard us and then ran when these guys showed up."

"Damn! So, someone else is looking for her?" Conner said.

"Looks like it."

"What if it's the FBI?" Jenna whispered the last three letters.

"I don't think the FBI would have been so clumsy," Terry answered.

"Who then?" Jenna asked.

"I don't know, but I think we need to find out."

Terry searched the rest of the camp and spotted something on the edge of the fire. He grabbed a stick and pulled out the corner of a burnt page from between two stones.

"Looks like a page someone printed out, like you'd do at home," he said after examining it.

He passed it around and they all looked at it. All of them shook their heads until Dawn recognised something. "Look, there, that's Dad and Selene's company logo."

Ryan leaned over to look. "Where?"

"There, clear as day."

"Clear as a foggy day maybe. Yeah, suppose it could be."

"It is, trust me," Dawn said. She pulled out her phone. "I'll find it, this was printed from their business website." A few taps later and Dawn showed them all the page, it matched exactly, and was filled with properties for sale, most of them islands.

"Do we think that's where she's ran to?" Jenna said. "I didn't know there were so many for sale."

"Yeah," Dawn nodded wisely. "A lot of people are moving away. This is prime selling season, but this year not many people are buying. I suppose a private island is not something rich folk are spending their money on this year." She had a sudden thought. "Terry, do you think you might have seen those two guys on Kneasley's yacht?"

Terry's eyes widened. "Yes, that's it, I think."

"Well, we have the videos, let's look through them and see if they're there."

"Ok, but I think we should get out of here first," Conner said, looking nervously around.

They all agreed it was a good idea. They went back to the 'eggy Su' and headed out to sea. They stopped on the edge of cover and scanned the area. Verbena might have been waiting out there, but there was no sign of her. Conner turned towards the harbor as Terry looked through the videos on his phone. After several minutes he found them.

"Here. That's definitely one of them, and that could be the other."

"Are they guests at the party?"

"No, they look like security."

"Interesting," Ryan said. "So Kneasley's security people are looking for Verbena as well. I wonder if she's stolen something from them?"

"They had that argument we heard," Dawn pointed out, "so we know something's not right."

"I suppose that means at least she won't be sabotaging anything for a while," Jenna said, "if she's gone into hiding."

Dawn scowled. "But we can't just let her get away with the things she's already done."

Conner sighed. "Then we've got to search all these islands to find her again."

Terry smiled. "Looks that way."

"Ok, but let's be smart about it."

Ryan grinned. "Business as usual then, Con."

CHAPTER TWELVE
SEASCAPE

TIDE OVER

A ship can generally move with the tide, but tide over is a specific maneuver involving floating the ship upriver on a rising tide, then anchoring or mooring up to resist the backwards push of the ebb tide.

The modern meaning has completely changed, and it now means to make do temporarily, to borrow money or goods against a short term problem, or to otherwise manage with less over a short period of time.

Of the ten properties listed on that particular web page, eight of them were islands. One of them had already been sold and two more of them were still occupied by the present owners. By asking their dad some subtle questions, Ryan and Dawn had worked out two of the remaining five had recently been viewed by potential buyers and no one had seen anything unusual, like a dirty brown boat. The teens put those to the bottom of the list and decided to explore the other three in order of distance from the shore, furthest first.

Rook Island, as it was called, wasn't much more than some grass and a few twisted trees on a rock about three hundred yards long and sixty yards wide. No one knew if the name came from the bird, a surname or indeed the chess piece. The teens had left early the day after Verbena had escaped, but it was still mid-morning by the time they arrived. It was the furthest east they'd ever been before. There was nothing beyond this point but the open ocean and, eventually, Europe. The island wasn't the most inviting of places; they could see why it hadn't been sold yet. A cool wind blew in from the sea almost constantly, bending the stunted trees over and leaving no place to shelter. The sea was much wilder here, darker and less forgiving. With nothing to stop them the waves were higher and arrived with greater force. Even on such a calm day, Conner was reluctant to take the 'eggy Su' around the windward side of the island. They checked it out anyway; Verbena was ex-military and might have been trained to survive in such a place. After circumnavigating the whole island and finding nothing, they quickly moved on.

The next island was further west, so the sea was more placid here. It was called Long Isle, one of many off the Maine coast with a similar name. It wasn't particularly long, which was possibly why it was called isle and not island. There were no trees at all here, just lots of low bushes and brambles. If someone was hiding here, they'd be difficult to find. Moving and concealing a whole boat was another matter. They drove around it anyway, checking the occasional inlet and rocky bay more closely. The edges of the island were surrounded by broken rock, much of it submerged. It was hazardous for their small boat, never mind anything with a deeper draft.

They found no sign of Verbena or anywhere she could have safely dragged her boat ashore. They were as certain as they could be she wouldn't have abandoned it. They did find some plastic waste, mostly bubble wrap, floating in a tide pool. They gathered up what they could of it and moved on again.

"I think she's here," Dawn said, showing her phone to the others. It was a satellite view of Ducknest Haven, the largest of the three islands and the only one with permanent buildings on it. "Look, there's a beach on this one. I think she likes beaches."

Ryan laughed. "How did you work that out? You hardly know her."

"Just a hunch. She obviously loves the sea, so why not beaches?"

"So," Conner said, "I'll head for the side of the island away from the beach, and then we sneak in."

"We know she can break into buildings, but I don't think she's in one of them, that would be too obvious," Dawn said studying the image.

Terry nodded. "I agree. She'll be camping out near her boat, ready to run. She'll be on edge, so we need to be very sneaky."

"But she needs to eat and drink," Jenna pointed out. "Unless her boat was already full of food and water, which is entirely possible."

"Yeah, she could have enough supplies for months on that boat," Ryan said.

"Do you think the Kneasleys' guys are still looking for her?" Conner asked.

"I'd bet they are," Ryan said, "so watch out for other boats."

"But they don't have the information we have, thanks to Terry." Conner smiled.

"So let's get her this time, before someone else does," Terry said very seriously.

Conner steered the boat in the general direction of Ducknest Haven, then more towards the north west side. From above, the island was shaped like a reversed comma with a wide tail. The end of the tail was to the southeast, where the beach sat in a narrow bay. The sea was calm and shallow here, and the same light blue-green as it was at Stonehaven. They all agreed this was the island they'd buy if they ever had enough money.

As the island was sometimes occupied, the vegetation was mostly trimmed and fairly regular. Grass, rows of trees and what looked like huge rose bushes grew everywhere on the island. There was no sign of any ducks, or their nests, although it could have been the wrong time of year for them. On the western edge, facing the mainland, a house had been built. It was a set of single story boxes clustered together with a separate boathouse to one side. There was no quay or harbor, but instead a concrete slipway and a hand winch. Everything was locked down tight with metal panels and stout padlocks. There was no 'for sale' sign but it matched the pictures on the website. With no other signs of life, smoke or boats, the teens had to go with Dawn's instinct and presume Verbena was on or near the beach, if she was here at all.

Around the edges of the island, the native plants had been left to grow. Pine trees and low bushes made up most of it, creating a corridor around which the teens could sneak. They were unable to land the 'eggy Su', nor find anywhere other than the beach where it was safe to moor up. They found a relatively calm inlet and Terry had to leap ashore while Conner held the boat bow first against a suitable rock using the motor. Terry then disappeared among the trees, emerging occasionally where the undergrowth thinned. Conner kept up with him as much as possible, the slight hum of the electric motor completely hidden by the sound of the waves on the rocks.

They were almost around to the beach by the time Terry reappeared and signalled them to stop. Conner steered in towards the island as close as he dared, the others watching out for rocks and other boats. Terry then disappeared again, and was gone for fifteen minutes or more. They were starting to worry he'd been spotted when he returned, gesturing them in to shore. He caught and held the bow line while they had a whispered conversation.

"I've found her," Terry said with a grin. "She's on the beach close to a huge rock that juts out into the sea. The boat is moored to the rocks at the end of the beach, and she's just sitting in the sun with a beer."

Dawn pulled out her phone and brought up the satellite photo. "Show us."

Terry zoomed in and pointed to a spot on the beach. The teens looked up and could see the actual rock formation Terry was indicating.

"We need to distract her, get her away from the boat so we can search it," Conner said, "see if we can find any decent evidence."

"Ok, I'll go around her and make a noise or something. Wait until she's out of sight before you move. And remember, she's good at this sort of thing, so be careful." Terry turned and disappeared again.

Conner headed for the end of the bay and waited on the other side of the rocks. The sea was swirling around here, but luckily it wasn't rough. He held the 'eggy Su' steady and waited, and then realised he didn't know when to move.

"When do I move in? We didn't agree a signal."

"I thought he was going to make a noise?" Ryan said, "just go then."

"What if I don't hear it?"

Dawn suddenly pointed. "He's there, he says go!" She pointed, but Terry had disappeared again by the time everyone else looked. Conner twisted the throttle to full and steered the boat around the rocks and in towards the beach. Sure enough, the brown boat was there, moored close to the rocks in water just deep enough to allow it to float when the tide was low. Planks were crudely tied to a series of plastic crates to form a temporary jetty. It wasn't the best way to moor a boat, but it did allow a relatively fast getaway.

Jenna was off the boat before it had even stopped, grabbing the bow line and pulling as hard as she could. Ryan and Dawn joined her and pulled until the boat grounded. Dawn and Jenna let go, leaving Ryan as a mooring point. Conner grinned at him and leapt onto the sand, then rushed over to join the others at the boat.

Dawn, Conner and Jenna approached the boat slowly, spreading out a little and heading for separate points. This close to it, they realised the boat wasn't much larger than the 'eggy Su'. It had a low deck at the rear and a raised cabin at the front. There was a small wheelhouse with a seat and a windshield to one side of a sliding hatch which led into the cabin. It was locked with a heavy-duty padlock. The deck was strewn with garbage, mainly beer bottles and take-out containers.

This close to it, they could see the boat wasn't actually dirty, but had been crudely painted with what could have been house paint. The original white showed through in places, and Jenna spotted the name of the craft as she approached the stern. The words 'Peace and Quiet' written in curly letters were just visible under the brown. The two outboard engines they were familiar with, or at least the sound of them, sat gleaming in the sun. They were relatively new and well maintained, and looked far too large for the size of the boat.

Jenna slowly inched along the planks and closer to a porthole and looked inside. There was just enough light filtering in through the other portholes to see the contents. The first thing she noticed was the mess. It was worse than the other four teen's bedrooms put together.

"Look at this," Jenna whispered. "What is all this stuff? I can't believe she sleeps in there. I want to get inside just to tidy up."

Dawn and Conner searched around the boat and on the deck. There wasn't much of interest on the outside apart from the odd beer bottle and a fire pit made from stones. Verbena hadn't left much evidence she had been there. Dawn and Conner joined Jenna. With their faces pressed against the glass the three tried to spot anything useful inside. Something that could be considered evidence and not junk.

"Look there," Jenna said, "sea balls, there must be ten dollars' worth."

"I can see maps and charts pinned to the wall, all the places she's been marked on them, like Matias and Teuila's place, and the harbor, maybe even the buoy locations," Dawn whispered.

"And look there, cuttings from the local newspaper, I can see headlines talking about the two fires." Conner smiled, "this boat is stuffed with evidence."

"Can we get inside?" Dawn asked.

"No," Ryan said, appearing suddenly behind them. "That's a serious lock. Unless any of you can pick it there's no chance of getting in there." He'd piled stones on the mooring line but kept one eye on their boat in case it pulled free. "We could break it off with a rock, maybe. But that would take time and make a noise."

"So then we report it to the police?"

"Maybe, do you think they'll take us seriously?"

"Possibly, we have a good track record."

Ryan laughed, "because of what happened last year?"

"Yes, they know we're serious."

A voice hissed at them from along a thin trail that meandered through the trees. "Agmeh yo." They all turned to see Terry standing only a few yards away.

"She's here?" Dawn asked.

"Alsoda!" Terry told them to get moving and they turned towards the 'eggy Su'.

Terry suddenly stopped, looking down at the sand. "You've left footprints all over. She'll know someone's been here."

"Can we scrub them out?" Conner asked.

"Too late, she's just up the trail. I think she's been using the toilet over at the house."

"We'll just have to go, she won't know who was here," Jenna said. "As long as she doesn't see the boat."

They all began to run back to the 'eggy Su' but Ryan stopped. "We need that evidence. If she sees someone's been here, she might destroy it or hide it somewhere else. Then we'll never find it."

"She's literally seconds away," Terry said firmly.

"Ok, get ready to move. Dawn, lend me a note pad."

"What for?"

"Dawn, there's no time."

"Ok, here's an old one."

Ryan took the notebook and headed back towards Verbena's boat. "Be ready to go, but don't leave without me."

The others weren't sure what his plan was, but only a few seconds later they heard a shout and Ryan was running back to the 'eggy Su', Verbena right behind him. Ryan had waited until the very last second to make sure Verbena saw him and was chasing after him.

"Go, go!" he yelled, running as fast as he could on the loose sand.

They all joined in and pushed the 'eggy Su' back into the sea. Conner jumped aboard and grabbed the throttle, flicking the on switch with familiar ease. This was another advantage of electric propulsion, there was no need to shut down the engine or start it up again, which was never an instant process.

Jenna leapt athletically into the boat and took her seat. She looked back with a worried expression as first Terry, then Dawn, jumped in after her. Ryan practically ran into the side of the boat, giving it a helpful boost and turning the bow before launching himself over the gunwale. He only made it halfway. Jenna grabbed his arm and helped him roll in the rest of the way, flicking cool seawater in all directions. His sneakers and the bottoms of his pant legs were soaked but he was grinning as he recovered and finally made it to his seat. Conner had already twisted the throttle to get them out of there.

When they looked back, Verbena was standing in the shallows, the waves breaking above her knees. She was red-faced and breathing heavily, silently glaring at them. Conner was sure she was about to dive in and try to grab the boat. He was convinced she'd make it. Instead, she took off back along the beach towards her own boat. Only seconds later they heard first one and then the second outboard roar into life.

Conner steered away from the beach and dangerous rocks and into the open sea, then turned towards the mainland, using his small compass to check the heading. "Ok, Ryan, what did you just do?"

The others turned to Ryan, who was grinning widely. "I stood next to the boat with one of Dawn's notebooks, trying to make it look like I'd taken it out of the boat. She obviously fell for it, and now she's chasing us to get it back." Ryan smirked and passed the notebook back to Dawn, who grabbed it and checked it for damage.

"So what now? Back to the harbor and call the police?"

"Exactly." Conner twisted the throttle almost as far as it would go and the 'eggy Su' sped up, skimming almost silently across the calm sea.

Behind them they could hear the two outboard engines revving up and down as Verbena moved away from her mooring.

"She'll have to be careful moving away from those rocks, but once she hits the open sea she'll soon catch up," Conner said, glancing over his shoulder.

Sure enough, only a few minutes later Verbena came powering towards them, gradually coming closer as the two powerful outboards bludgeoned their way through the swell.

"Is this as fast as she'll go?" Ryan asked Conner.

"No, we don't want to get too far ahead. We want her to chase us but not catch us, right?"

"Right. But she's gaining on us so you might want to give it a bit more."

"Ok, but the battery charge is going down fast as it is. I don't want to flatten the battery now."

"I really must look into upgrading the motor and batteries," Ryan said, mainly to himself. "I wonder if we can fit two motors back there?"

"Not really the time to be thinking about upgrades, Ry." Conner said. "Let's deal with this situation first."

They all looked back and watched as Verbena slowly edged closer.

CHAPTER THIRTEEN

SEA BATTLE

BITTER END

*A bitt is a bollard or post fastened to a pier or ship
and used for tying the mooring lines to. The end of the line
that is attached to the bitt is called the bitter end. A sailor
pulling in the line would eventually reach the bitter end.*

*The term has now extended to mean hanging on
or continuing until the very last possible moment during
adverse or impossible situations.*

It was a long way back to the harbor, at least an hour, but it seemed they'd made Verbena angry and she pursued them all the way across the sea and back towards the shore. Mile after mile the sound of her outboard motors followed closely behind, grumbling like angry bears. Although they couldn't hear her, they imagined Verbena making a similar noise inside the wheelhouse. They all thought Verbena would eventually come to her senses, break off the chase and go back into hiding, but she relentlessly pursued them as if her life depended on it. Even when the harbor came into view, and other boats with potential witnesses on them began to appear, she carried on.

So far, Kneasley's security people hadn't shown up. If they did, the teens weren't certain she'd run again. There was a chance she'd stand and fight, and possibly win. If she did decide to escape, they doubted they'd ever see her again.

Although they weren't very far from the harbor now, it seemed like miles to the teens as they led Verbena's boat ever closer. She wasn't very far behind them; they could see her red hair and the occasional gesture she made in their direction.

"Can we call the police yet?" Dawn asked, "I have a weak signal, might be enough."

"If you steer closer to the beach, Conner, we should get a better signal," Ryan said.

"Don't make any sudden movements; if she gets suspicious, she'll just head off and we'll never find her again," Terry said, looking back towards their pursuer.

"Good point," Conner agreed, "we don't want to lose her now."

"How's the battery holding up?" Ryan asked.

"Er, well, it's low," Conner admitted.

"Are we going to make it to the harbor?"

"Probably, as long as we don't have to go any faster or start doing any evasive maneuvers."

"Look, what's she doing?" Jenna pointed at Verbena, who was climbing onto the cabin roof.

"Get down!" Terry shouted, ducking his head and grabbing a paddle to use as a shield. "She's got a spear gun!"

The others dived off their seats and scrambled to copy Terry, grabbing at the nearest paddle. Conner couldn't let go of the tiller and there were no paddles left, so he sat on the floor of the boat and hid behind the motor as best he could.

After a short pause, there was a sound like a sudden release of air and something thudded into the transom. There was a yell of triumph and the 'eggy Su' slowed a little.

Conner risked a look around. "She's caught us with the spear. Look!"

The others lowered their paddles and looked. A fishing spear was lodged in the transom and a line ran from it to Verbena's ship. She was holding the line and trying to tie it off.

Conner twisted the throttle to full power then began to zig-zag through the waves. On his third zag, the spear gun flew from Verbena's hand and the 'eggy Su' shot forwards. Just before they were free and clear, the spear gun hit the bow rail of Verbena's ship and hitched itself around it.

Conner began to slow down to see if it would release itself.

"No, keep going," Terry shouted.

"What? we're caught!" Conner yelled back.

Terry smiled, "no, she's caught."

It took Conner a few seconds to work out what Terry was talking about, then the penny dropped. He twisted the throttle a little to keep up the tension and carried on towards the harbor.

On board Verena's boat, she realized what was happening. She reversed her engines and began to slow the 'eggy Su'. Conner twisted the throttle as far as it would go and then tried to twist it more. The powerful electric motor whirred and stopped their backwards motion, but the charge level began to drop alarmingly fast. "This might be the time for someone to call 911!" Conner yelled.

"Oh, yes, I'm on it," Jenna pulled out her phone and began tapping on it.

Dawn pulled out her own phone and began recording the whole thing, something they should have been doing for several minutes.

The roaring of the outboards stopped and the two boats surged forwards. Conner watched as Verbena approached the bow rail and tried to untangle the speargun. Conner began to zig-zag again, throwing Verbena off-balance and triggering a torrent of words she must have learned in the navy. She managed to brace herself and try again, but there wasn't enough slack in the rope.

Jenna had got through to the police, cell-phone reception now strong enough as they neared the shore.

"Hello, yes. Er, we have a bit of a situation. We're in a boat just out from the harbor. Someone in another boat has fired a spear gun at us and we're attached to it. The person on the other boat is almost certainly responsible for several crimes. No, I'm serious. Jenna Cushman. Yes. No. If they head for the harbor, they'll find us. Ok."

Jenna put her phone away and turned to explain to the others. "They've notified the coastguard and the local police; they should both be here soon."

Dawn suddenly shouted a warning, "Conner, look out!"

They all turned to see Verbena lying against the bow rail and pulling on the rope, gathering it in hand over hand, her face a mask of anger. The two boats slowly moved closer. Conner zig-zagged again, but Verbena was too strong and too well-braced to shake off.

"Cut the rope!" Terry yelled.

Ryan looked over the transom towards where the spear was stuck. "it's metal, I can't reach the rope."

"Knock it out, with the paddle," Dawn yelled.

Ryan grabbed his paddle from the bottom of the boat and leaned over, bashing at the spear. The barbed tip was deep in the wood, but the spear bent slightly when he hit it. He lifted the paddle to try again, Verbena only a few yards away now. "Keep going, I just need one good hit," Ryan said.

Verbena's hands were red with rope burns, but she persisted, using all of her strength to pull the line in. Despite this, she was smiling. "Got you, little sneaks! Give it back or I'll drag this stupid boat out to the shipping lanes and leave you there." She slackened the rope a little and stood, then tied the rope securely to the bow rail. She glared at them, tall and proud, triumphant.

The sound of sirens could be heard in the distance, getting louder by the second. Red and blue lights could be seen approaching the harbor, seemingly from all directions. Verbena swore, turned around and headed for the wheelhouse. She was going to run for it and the 'eggy Su' was still firmly attached.

Conner stood on the rear thwart and pulled a small knife out of his pocket. Now the two boats where close enough, he could reach the rope easily. The knife wasn't sharp, only a few of the braided strands parted as he cut it. "This is going to take too long; I need more time!"

There was whooshing noise and something flew over his head. A loud crack followed and then the sound of Verbena screaming and falling over into a pile of assorted junk.

Conner tried not to look at what at happened, he just concentrated on slicing the rope. Strand by strand the rope peeled apart until finally the last part gave and the 'eggy Su' was free. Conner glanced up at Verbena's boat and was surprised to see one of the paddles embedded in the windscreen. He turned around and saw Jenna, standing up and holding another paddle, ready to throw it if needed.

"Good shot!" Conner said.

Jenna blushed slightly, "thanks."

Conner was about to just let go of the cut end of the spear gun line, but had a better idea. Instead, he threw the line into the sea directly in front of Verbena's boat. It was something of a long shot, but worth a try.

After a few seconds of cursing, Verbena recovered and came storming towards the bow rail. Whatever she was about to do was forgotten when she saw Conner letting go of the cut line. She looked around her boat, grabbed the anchor and threw it onto the 'eggy Su'. It landed in the bottom of the boat between Dawn and Conner, its chain rode trailing back to Verbena's boat. She rushed back to her wheelhouse and reversed her engines with a loud roar. She turned away from them and headed out to sea as fast as she could.

"I can't move it!" Dawn gasped, trying to lift the anchor and throw it overboard before the rode tightened. The anchor was a simple pole with a split blade at the bottom. The rode pulled tight as Verbena moved away and the blades slid under the rear thwart and jammed in place. The 'eggy Su' began to move backwards, her flat stern pushing against the water.

This extra drag slowed Verbena down, but she increased the power and carried on moving.

Conner twisted the throttle to full and the two boats slowed a little. Although the electric motor was more than a match for the speed of the outboards, it just didn't have the same power.

"Con, wait, save the power," Ryan said. "I've got an idea."

Conner released the throttle and the 'eggy Su' increased speed, the hull dipping and splashing water into the boat.

"Look," Ryan pointed. "At the end of the chain there's nylon rope. We can pull the rode in like Verbena did and cut it."

Conner and Dawn leaned over and grabbed the chain rode. It was a little rusty and slimy, but they managed to pull it far enough for first Ryan, then Jenna and Terry to grab hold of. They all pulled together and slowly reeled in the chain. Their extra weight on the stern caused it to dip further into the sea and water poured over the transom. The extra drag slowed them down and caused Verbena to start shouting again. Terry and Jenna moved backwards once they had enough chain, causing the boat to rebalance and bringing the nylon part of the rode close enough for Conner to start cutting. The join between the rope and the chain was a tangled mess of knots, so they pulled a little more chain until they had a single strand. Conner began to cut the nylon, sawing with all his strength until it finally parted and they all fell backwards off their seats.

Verbena's boat leapt forwards now it was unburdened. She looked back towards the teens, shrugged and then waved goodbye. It looked like she was going to escape again. A few yards later, the entire bow rail, spear gun and all, was yanked off into the sea and underneath the boat as the trailing rope wrapped around one of her propellers. Loud bangs and cracks were heard under the boat as the spear gun and rail followed the rope. The port engine stalled with a deep buzzing sound that turned into a metallic grinding. Smoke began to pour from the engine as the noise grew louder. The starboard engine slammed over to full lock and stayed in that position and the boat began to turn in a wide circle. Verbena came out of the wheelhouse to look at the engines. She kicked them a few times, then disappeared into the main cabin.

Another sound became noticeable above the clatter of Verbena's outboards. Terry shouted a warning and they all looked towards where he was pointing. A small but rapid speedboat was heading directly towards them with two people inside it. At first, they all thought it was coming to help and so didn't react. There was a flicker of orange light as the person in the passenger seat ignited a cloth tied to a small bottle. The boat turned towards Verbena's and the passenger stood up, one hand on the windshield, the other ready to throw the flaming bottle.

"Gasoline bomb!" Terry shouted. "They're trying to burn the boat!"

Just as the man threw the bottle the speedboat hit the wake created by the remaining outboard and the bottle fell short, landing harmlessly in the sea. The speedboat circled around and the man could be seen preparing another bottle.

Conner turned the 'eggy Su' towards the speed boat and headed straight for it. "We have to stop them; we need that evidence!"

Jenna looked back towards the harbor. She could see all the flashing lights and hear the sirens, but there was no sign of the coastguard or anyone else coming out to help. "Looks like we're on our own, for now."

There was still no sign of Verbena, but they didn't for one second think she'd given up. The speedboat was now approaching from the outside of the foaming circle formed by the wake, trying to get alongside the boat so they couldn't miss. Conner did the same, guiding the 'eggy Su' in behind them. The speedboat was much faster than either of the other boats, but had to slow down to match Verbena's speed.

As Conner got into position, Ryan grabbed one of the oars and held it out like he was holding a jousting lance. As the 'eggy Su' came alongside it, Ryan struck at the man, aiming for the bottle in his hand. As both of the boats were moving his aim was off and the oar struck the passenger seat instead.

The attack by the almost silent electric boat surprised the man as he was about to throw another bottle. He stumbled sideways and almost fell overboard, grabbing the gunwales and letting go of the bottle, which hit the side and dropped into the sea. He recovered quickly and glared at the teens. He sat down and a few seconds later an orange flame showed the men had come prepared.

The speedboat moved towards Verbena's boat again, lining up for a shot as close as they could get. The passenger lifted the bottle, glancing around to see where the 'eggy Su' was. Conner had dropped back a little and now approached again. He wondered just how many of the bottle bombs these people had.

At the last minute the man changed targets, spinning around and launching the flaming bottle straight towards the 'eggy Su'. Ryan was ready with the oar and he lifted it to deflect the bottle. It smashed on the end of the oar with a burst of orange flames and glass, some of which reached Ryan. He quickly plunged the oar into the sea and the flames went out.

"You ok?" Dawn asked, worry fighting with anger on her face.

"I'm good, but let's not do that again."

The man was already lighting up another bottle as Conner backed off a little. The battery light was flashing amber now; they had only a few more minutes of power left. Conner was determined to make them count. "Everyone, hold on to something."

"Oh damn, what's he going to do?" Ryan laughed nervously.

Conner throttled up the 'eggy Su' and headed for the speedboat. Instead of aiming at it, he pulled alongside then quickly turned, sending up a rooster tail of water that landed in the speedboat and all over the two occupants. The flame on the bottle the man was holding went out. He cursed and tried to light it again, but his lighter was also wet. The man lifted the bottle anyway and threw it towards Verbena's boat. Another followed, and then more. At least a couple of them landed on the rear deck and smashed. None of them were lit, but now the second man had produced a flare gun and was passing it to his passenger. Determined to get the job done, the speedboat moved in until it was hull to hull with Verbena's boat.

At that point, Verbena emerged looking extremely annoyed. She lifted her arm and pointed it towards the speedboat. She had a slingshot catapult in her hand, the elastic stretched back to her cheek. The windshield of the speedboat shattered moments later, making the man drop back into his seat. The flare gun went off, the hot flare bouncing off Verbena's shoulder and dropping to the deck. The gasoline ignited and the boat was engulfed in flames.

To everyone's surprise, Verbena leapt from her own boat and onto the speedboat, landing with a crack behind the seats. She quickly found her balance and grabbed each of the men around the neck, squeezing and lifting and swearing all kinds of vengeance on the two men and their families.

The teens watched in horror as the boat burned, the fire taking hold quickly on the gasoline soaked garbage.

"Do the water thing!" Dawn cried, "put the fire out!"

Ryan reached over and gripped her shoulder. "Can't do that Dant, it's gasoline, it will just spread."

The battery warning light flashed red a few times and the engine whirred down to silence. Conner, despite the evidence, twisted the throttle back and forth a few times, but the batteries were completely drained. The teens sat, dead in the water, drifting with the tide as the brown boat continued to circle, creating a white wake and trailing red flames and clouds of smoke.

A few minutes later the Sea Fox appeared, with several police officers on deck. They saw the familiar figure of Aksel standing with them; he was waving and looking concerned. They headed straight for Verbena's boat, which was slowing down. Both engines were now giving off black smoke. One of the crew stopped the brown boat with a gaff and another sprayed it with white foam. The flames on the deck went out, but more could be seen inside the cabin.

In the distance, a Coastguard helicopter had arrived and was chasing down the small speedboat. It seemed Verbena and the two men had formed a temporary alliance and were making a run for the open sea.

Dawn looked at the others, "is it over?"

Terry shrugged, "seems to be."

"Hopefully the police can find something intact on that boat," Jenna said, "if it hasn't all burnt to ashes."

Ryan, blood seeping from some of the cuts on his face, stepped over to the motor and took hold of the rudder handle. "Right Con, your turn to do some work for a change."

Conner smiled but moved over to Ryan's seat and took up one of the remaining paddles. He Terry and Jenna started to move them back to the harbor and the inevitable broadside of questions from the police, parents and other interested parties.

Ryan looked under his seat at the anchor lodged there. "Well, at least we've got a proper anchor now. Try not to lose this one, Con."

EPILOGUE

I t was nearing the end of their summer break when they finally found out what evidence the police had recovered from Verbena's boat, or at least the information reported on by the local media and by talking to Aksel, Matias and Teuila. Their involvement in the police investigation had been brief and occurred during the first few days after Verbena's arrest. After all their hard work, and a brief recap of their activities, it seemed they were no longer required. They had mixed feelings about the situation; they certainly didn't want to spend the rest of their vacation inside hot police-stations and courthouses, but it would have been nice to be recognized for what they'd done.

It appeared that Verbena had made the most of her time in the boat's cabin while the two men tried to set it alight. She'd gathered up as much of her evidence as possible and thrown it into a metal chest, which had survived the fire intact. Unfortunately, the same evidence was used to convict her of arson and property damage. The brown boat also turned out to be stolen, and she also admitted to several other crimes including stealing food and gasoline.

Ryan's wounds were superficial, just a few shallow cuts that quickly healed. His hair was badly scorched at the front but it soon grew back. The two men were found guilty of assault and sent to jail. They refused to give up the name of the person who had hired them.

The teens had decided to get the pieces of their new boat finished before they returned to school, so they'd made camp at the prof's island for the whole weekend. Hopefully, as soon as they returned next year, and if there were no mysteries to solve, they could begin assembling it straight away and have the whole summer to learn to sail. Although the topics of conversation were often about normal teenage things, like parents, teachers, pizza toppings, games, and movies, they couldn't help but return to talking about the investigation occasionally.

"It's ironic," Conner said, studying the list of parts attached to a clipboard.

"It certainly is," Ryan agreed.

"What is?" Dawn said impatiently.

"What did we use to help us bail the water out when the 'eggy Su' was sabotaged?"

"Plastic bottles."

"Exactly. I wouldn't have been able to cut glass bottles with my knife, so plastic helped us."

The others nodded; it was certainly something to think about.

"I don't know how you can be so calm about it all," Dawn said into the silence, "Verbena was aiming that spear gun at you, I saw it."

Conner put down his clipboard. "Well, the court said not. She's some kind of spear-fishing expert, apparently, even had a witness to prove it. She claims she can hit anything she aims at, and as she hit the transom that's where she was aiming. The judge believed her, so, what can I say?"

"Hmm, I'm not convinced. I don't think she cared what she hit as long as the boat stopped."

"I was more concerned about when she cut a hole in the 'eggy Su'," Conner said. "It was on the list of charges against her, but then it was never mentioned again. And Verbena throwing a heavy anchor at us didn't even make it that far."

"Not enough evidence Con, even we couldn't say for sure it was Verbena who damaged the boat, and we got a free anchor!" Ryan said. "She's back in jail now anyway, so she got what she deserved."

"I can't believe she turned on the Kneasleys so quickly," Jenna said. "She'd saved every piece of evidence; it was like she'd planned to blackmail them from day one."

"For all the good it did," Terry said, "the judge threw most of it out. They got off lightly, as usual."

"I wouldn't say 'lightly'," Conner said, "the council members had to resign, so they lost their contacts, and the solar farm is postponed, so they bought an expensive field for nothing."

Dawn smiled, "and now Aksel and Matias and Teuila can move forwards with their projects, which is great."

"What were you and prof talking about earlier, Con?" Ryan asked, changing the subject.

"You know that marine reserve I've been talking about? The prof's offered to help me with it, and to propose Rogue Island as either one edge or the center point."

"That's great!"

"Yeah, let's hope the council see it that way and aren't too hostile."

"Don't see why they should be," Jenna pointed out, "it was only the bad ones who had to resign."

"Maybe they were friends, or related. Some people hold a grudge for a long time."

Dawn pulled out a notepad. "So, how many sea balls have we got? The last total was seventeen."

Terry produced a couple more and Jenna had one.

"Twenty?" Dawn complained, "you know they released thousands?"

"Twenty dollars is better than nothing," Ryan shrugged.

"Not going to get us a solar panel though," Conner said.

"No, but it's a start."

"I wonder what will happen next summer?" Dawn mused.

"I'll bet the Kneasleys will be involved," Terry said.

"No doubt," Dawn nodded.

"We're experts now," Ryan laughed, "we'll have the case solved in a few days, whatever it is, and then we're free to take our new boat out."

Conner smiled, "sounds good. But we haven't built it yet, so get back to work."

"Yes, boss!" They all chorused.

"That's captain to you."

ABOUT THE AUTHORS

Author **Steve Wedlock** has lived a literal personal life afloat on the sea, with more than 350,000 nautical miles as master of many types of vessels, a Marine surveyor, a builder of schooners, a teacher of seamanship, navigation, and boat handling, and sea captain. Born and raised on the coast of Maine, this life became a part of him early on as a child—running around on the shore and rocks, fishing off lobster floats, and getting involved in boating as a youth. Steve's vast background in oceanic living brought him to want to share his knowledge and love of the sea and sparked his inspiration to share his stories. In the early 1970s, Steve wrote a private collection of seamanship subjects—weather lore, navigation, ship handling, systems—for his crew. Steve believes that interesting settings and realistic and relatable characters are what make a great children's story. A plot that has intrigue and protagonists that have conflict keep young readers engaged. *The League of Maritime Adventurers: The Ungrateful Rescue* is his debut middle-grade/young adult book in this series. He hopes that his book's young readers gain interest in the shores and oceans and that it encourages them to explore on their own with their friends. When Steve isn't writing thrilling mystery adventure stories for children, he enjoys a hobby in photography, using vintage cameras. He is currently retired and based in Antequera, Spain, spending three months a year visiting family in the United States, and another three months exploring new places in the world.

Steve Dean was born and still lives in the city of Nottingham in the UK. He began to read at a very early age and soon became an avid consumer of genre fiction. Over the years, he tried several jobs before ending up in IT support. During this time, Steve began writing his own fiction, eventually becoming a full-time freelancer. When not dreaming up strange monsters and robots, Steve plays tabletop and video role-playing games far too much, watches science fiction and science fact, and reads from his ever-growing library of genre novels. Just for a change, he also grows cacti and house plants, makes furniture, and tinkers with technology.

www.ingramcontent.com/pod-product-compliance
Lightning Source LLC
Chambersburg PA
CBHW020256130626
46549CB00005B/2240

* 9 781737 985426 *